PRAISE FOR THE SERIES

"The perfect mystery to read with a glass of *vino* in hand."

—*Shelf Awareness*, starred review

"Light and enjoyable… If you feel like taking an armchair tour of France, they hit just the right spot."

—*Mystery Scene Magazine*

"Masterful."

—*Star Tribune*

"Beautifully done."

—*Bookloons*

"Decadent, delicious, and delightful, the Winemaker Detective series blends an immersion in French countryside, winemaking, and gourmet attitude with mystery and intrigue."

—*Wine Industry Network Advisor*

"A fun and informative take on the cozy crime mystery, French style."

—*Eurocrime*

"It is easy to see why this series has a following. The descriptive language is captivating... crackling, interesting dialogue, and persona."

—*Foreword Reviews*

"The authors of the Winemaker Detective series hit that mark each and every time."

—*Student of Opinions*

"Francophiles, history buffs, mystery fans, oenophiles will want to add the entire series to their reading shelf."

—*The Discerning Reader*

"Intrigue and plenty of good eating and drinking... will whet appetites of fans of both *Iron Chef* and *Murder, She Wrote*."

—*Booklist*

"One of my favorite series to turn to when I'm looking for something cozy and fun!"

—*Back to Books*

"Wine lovers and book lovers, for a perfect break in the shadows of your garden or under the sun on the beach, get a glass of wine, and enjoy this cozy mystery. Even your gray cells will enjoy!"

—*Library Cat*

"Recommended for those who like the journey, with good food and wine, as much as the destination."

—*Writing About Books*

"The reader is given a fascinating look into the goings on in the place the story is set and at the people who live there, not to mention all the wonderful food and drinks."

—*The Book Girl's Book Blog*

"A quick, entertaining read. It reminds me a bit of a good old English Murder Mystery such as anything by Agatha Christie."

—*New Paper Adventures*

"I love good mysteries. I love good wine. So imagine my joy at finding a great mystery about wine, and winemaking, and the whole culture of that fascinating world."

—William Martin, *New York Times* bestselling author

"It is best consumed slightly chilled, and never alone. You will be intrigued by its mystery, and surprised by its finish, and it will stay with you for a very long time."

—*Peter May*

THE WINEMAKER DETECTIVE SERIES

www.lefrenchbook.com/winemaker-detective-series/

Want to read more for free?
Read your way to France
Get your discovery pack:
www.lefrenchbook.com/read-your-way-to-france

Foul Play
in
Vouvray

A Winemaker Detective Mystery

Jean-Pierre Alaux & Noël Balen

Translated and adapted by
Sally Pane and Amy Richards

*It is well to remember
that there are five reasons for drinking:
the arrival of a friend,
one's present or future thirst,
the excellence of the wine,
or any other reason.*

— Latin proverb

1

"Cut!"

The cameramen, lighting technicians, boom operator, grips, and cast stood at attention, awaiting the director's next order.

David Navarre took his eyes off Simone when he heard muttering in a corner of the soundstage. The actor searched for the unruly crew member and found him, just as he was leaning into another technician and opening his mouth again.

"Would the pudgy little martinet get on with it!" The crew member's voice was hushed but loud enough to draw snickers from the handful of people nearby.

David held his breath, hoping Max Armond hadn't heard. The atmosphere was strained already.

He hadn't. Armond rose from his chair and approached Simone, who, holding a rumpled silk sheet over her bare breasts, had pulled herself upright on the daybed. "Finally, you gave me some thing worth a hard-on," he said, running his stubby fingers through his greasy thinning hair. "I was beginning to wonder whether you had it in you." He grunted and started walking away. "Break for lunch!"

Simone, still clutching the sheet, reached for a robe and wrapped it around herself. Only her shaking hands and pursed lips betrayed her. She locked eyes with David as she got up. Then she turned on her heel and left the soundstage.

The scene had been grueling. Armond's demands were fanatical. The director, true to his reputation, had bullied Simone mercilessly. "Get your panties out of their little knot and loosen up! I need a bitch, not a priss! Can you do it or not?"

David had been sorely tempted to intervene. But Simone, his twenty-two-year-old lover, would have to make her own way if she wanted to get to the top and stay there.

David gave the head camera operator a nod and escaped to his trailer. His status had secured him a haven the size of small home, with a full bathroom, spacious bedroom, paneled wardrobe area, lounge with leather seating, multiple flat screens, fully-stocked bar, and fresh flowers daily.

The producer had taken pains to rent it after receiving the actor's list of demands.

A cinematic giant, David Navarre was an indulged man. But he was also affable and approachable. He always had a pleasant word for the makeup artist, a pat on the back for the technicians, a complicit wink for the lighting designer, and a generosity of spirit for novice actors who were nervous about going face-to-face with him.

He stretched out on his leather sofa and closed his eyes, his cell phone on his chest. As he had expected, the phone pinged.

It was Simone, texting from her trailer: "What a prick."

"Yeah, baby," he tapped back. "But you nailed it."

"Think so?"

"Yeah, I do."

"What about that last line? Did I sound too sultry?"

"How could you sound too sultry? It was perfect, just like Armond said. Now get some rest. We've got to go back out there."

David put the phone back on his chest and closed his eyes again. Simone was handling herself admirably, despite Armond's tirades. The famed director was a man who pushed his stars to their limit. He also enjoyed feeling up the young women who were eager to work with him. That would get him in trouble someday. The Time's Up and Me Too movements were grabbing the headlines in the United States, and now they were in the news in France, as well. A sexual-harassment hotline had been set up at the Cannes Film Festival. The festival's tote bags contained fliers warning that such misconduct could lead to fines and even imprisonment. There had even been a rally on the red carpet.

Armond's hour of reckoning would come. But not today. David got up and poured himself a drink. Later, he'd promise Simone a trip to Dior when filming was wrapped up.

Some gossips claimed that his lover owed her first major roles to the art of selective sex. Her previous boyfriends included a fifty-year-old Italian producer, a former Brazilian Formula One racer, a Golden-Globe-winning Hollywood director, and the vice president of a television network.

Her relatively recent romance with David had provided the celebrity websites and tabloids with multiple photographs, while their twenty-eight-year age difference had added fuel to speculation that Simone was a user.

Most certainly, she was drawn to mature, powerful, and wealthy men who offered security and experience. No one, however, knew her the way he did. Despite Simone's proud and vivacious exterior, she questioned her looks and talent and seemed compulsive about proving herself.

It was this uncertainty that brought out David's protective instincts and gnawed at him at the same time. He pretended to ignore her penchant for flirting—an attempt to show she could captivate any man of her choosing, even as she bristled at being taken for just another hot starlet. But he hated it. David, who had seduced and left more women than he cared to count, was smitten. And for the first time in his life, he himself was feeling insecure. Did Simone love him, or would she drop him as soon as she didn't need him anymore?

He was ruminating on this when his cell phone rang. He looked at the screen and answered.

"Well, well! What a surprise! Mr. Cooker, the master winemaker himself! And to what do I owe this unexpected call? I had given up hope. I've been waiting for ages for you to come to Touraine… I know. I won't hold it against you. You're very busy, I know… I know… An American production company wants to do a documentary on you? Ah, I suspected you wouldn't be coming just to see me. Be careful, though. Don't give away too much about how you work. Remember *Mondovino*—that fucking movie, clever, very clever, realistic and misleading at the same time, very negative... The camera can screw you. I know what I'm talking about. Not that I need to tell *you* this, but watch out with the Americans. They can be cagey."

The actor reached for his bottle of whiskey but thought better of it. He had to be back on set soon.

"Of course!" he said, nodding. "Uh-huh... Listen, it's simple. While they're filming this documentary, you'll have a little free time, correct? If you could look at the parcel I told you about, I'd be in your debt. I want to get that land back in shape. They tell me it hasn't been plowed for decades. Can you believe it? And then I'd like you to help me with my wine. I'll never be able to launch my vintage without your advice and support. When exactly do you get here? Saturday? Perfect. I'm giving a little party for some friends at the château. Will you come?"

Another silence. David changed his mind and poured himself a drink. He had to face Armond again.

"Listen, Benjamin, I know it's not your thing, but I insist. It will be very nice, you'll see. Of course, you can bring a guest. Bring more than one. I insist!"

2

Under a light early-afternoon rain, Benjamin Cooker and his assistant, Virgile Lanssien, left the banks of the Garonne River in Bordeaux. A last-minute consultation at the Cooker & Co. offices on the Allées de Tourny and a deluge of test results in the lab had delayed their planned mid-morning departure. Finally free, Benjamin, France's preeminent authority on wine, sloughed off his tension as he slipped behind the wheel of his Mercedes. He was looking forward to this getaway.

The sky had cleared by the time they got to Poitiers, and a warm spring sun accompanied them all the way to Touraine. They drove along the Loire River, following its slow, somewhat somnolent course. After going through Amboise, they turned right, onto a narrow ribbon of blacktop. Château de Pray, with its twin towers and clean white shutters, rose up before them, rooted firmly on a hillside of verdant terraces. A smiling staff member, whom Benjamin had met during a previous stay, was waiting on the steps.

Whenever Benjamin came to the Loire Valley, he had the luxury of choice. There was the graceful and charming Château de la Tortinière, near Montbazen. It was run by Anne Olivereau and her husband, Xavier, fourth-generation hoteliers. The mansion, with its expansive lawn, was a place whose peace and tranquility Benjamin appreciated. In fact, he had had a lengthy stay there once, when he was recovering from a mugging in Paris.

On the other hand, he found it hard to resist the imposing Château de Pray, formerly run by the radiant Graziella Laurenty and her husband, Ludovic, one of the region's most creative chefs. The Michelin-starred restaurant was now headed by Frederic Brisset, who was known for cuisine that was balanced, flavorful, and executed with finesse. Benjamin admired his infusions, as well as his seafood dishes, almost all of which showcased produce sourced from markets in Amboise and Tours.

Benjamin and Virgile climbed out of the convertible and stretched in the sunlight. Virgile let out a loud yawn.

Benjamin frowned before beaming at the staff member, Agathe, who was crossing the courtyard to greet them. "Let's not look like we're bored before we even say hello," he grumbled.

"Sorry, boss. Couldn't help it. Busy morning."

"And probably an equally busy night before that," Benjamin muttered.

Reaching them, Agathe extended her hand. "Gentlemen, you both look tired."

"Yes, I'm afraid we are," Benjamin said. "It's not a long drive, but we had a hectic morning. I'm happy we're finally here. Have you met my assistant? Actually, calling Virgile an assistant doesn't do him justice. He's my indispensable right-hand man."

"Indispensable? Now that's a supreme compliment."

"It was Sir Robert Baden-Powell who said, 'If you make yourself indispensable to your employer, he's not going to part with you in a hurry.'"

Agathe turned to Virgile. "Given the esteem Mr. Cooker holds you in, I look forward to getting to know you better."

Benjamin cleared his throat, surreptitiously warning Virgile. This wasn't the time for any of his flirting.

Virgile gave him an innocent look. "Who, me?" he mouthed silently.

"Three TV people are waiting for you in the little salon," Agathe said, either ignoring her guests' exchange or oblivious to it. "They arrived about an hour ago. I served them coffee and *madeleines*."

"I appreciate your hospitality," Benjamin said, pulling his bags from the trunk of the car. "By the way, how's Chef Brisset?"

"He's fine. He's at the market now, buying asparagus. They're marvelous this year."

They left their luggage at the reception desk and entered the salon. A fiftyish woman and two men barely in their thirties were seated in front of an imposing nineteenth-century fireplace. Seeing them, the woman got up. Liza Stechelmann, the director from Open Air Entertainment, gave Benjamin and Virgile solid handshakes and introduced her colleagues: Fabrice, a tall, muscular cameraman with a large knot of hair on top of his head, and Hugo, the shorter and slimmer soundman.

Benjamin ordered a pot of tea and studied Liza's every gesture as she explained the filming schedule. She was a woman with a piercing gaze, alternately impertinent and insecure. Benjamin perceived a defensiveness that cloaked a lingering melancholy. He listened patiently, speaking only when he was sure she was done.

"There's one thing I need to clarify," he said.

"Tell me."

"I'm very flattered that you're interested in our work, but I'm not sure I understand the exact nature of your project."

"What do you want to know?"

"Open Air is an independent production company filming a documentary that will be aired in the United States? And one of your offices is in Paris?"

"Exactly," Liza answered, narrowing her eyes. "I've already explained that. I've been very upfront about my intentions, and I cannot film if I don't have your complete confidence."

"Of course," Benjamin said, pouring his Darjeeling into a white porcelain cup. "I'm aware of everything you've told me, but I must let you know that I've done my research. Your work is highly praised, and you've received quite a few awards. Some critics even say you're one of the best documentary filmmakers of your generation."

"Thank you." Liza smiled, although her brown eyes still held a hint of doubt.

"I've been told you're honest, as well. My only concern regarding this film project is…"

"Don't be afraid to talk frankly."

"I'm not afraid, Ms. Stechelmann. It's not my nature. I simply want to offer the most accurate portrayal of our craft. The wine world is complex, and the general public knows relatively little about the role of an oenologist and even less about what a winemaker does. Do you understand? We should hide nothing, dodge no questions, and avoid any conflations, clichés, and shortcuts."

"That's exactly our intention, Mr. Cooker, and to that end we have chosen the ideal format."

"Ninety minutes, right?"

"Yes. Most of my documentaries are sixty minutes. To get sufficient footage, we may need two weeks of filming."

"That much time?" Virgile asked.

"If we can, we'll wrap it up more quickly."

Benjamin reached for his assistant's cup and emptied the teapot, waiting for Liza to elaborate.

"Starting tomorrow, we'll do some takes on location so that you can get used to filming and feel comfortable," she said. "We should head out first thing after breakfast. The light is often very good at that hour. Right, Fabrice?"

Fabrice nodded.

"Not too early, though," said Benjamin. "We've been invited to a reception tonight at David

Navarre's estate, and we might not get back to the hotel before midnight."

"David Navarre, the actor? You didn't tell me."

"No, he invited us after we made our arrangements with you. I've been putting him off in regard to a dormant piece of land he's hoping to revive for the production of a special vintage. The gathering tonight is a perfect opportunity to discuss it and lay the groundwork."

"Would he agree to be filmed while you're checking out his parcel?"

"I don't know," Benjamin said. "I'd have to ask him."

"It would be a great boon for our project. Footage with a celebrity of his caliber would generate a lot of buzz."

"I agree, but it all depends on his availability. He's a very busy man, and he happens to be making a movie."

"If that's the case, perhaps we could film you at the party tonight?"

Benjamin caught himself before saying anything too quickly. He was irritated by her attempt to insinuate herself into a part of his private life that he had no intention of revealing. He took a diplomatic tack instead. "It's awkward. I wouldn't want to give a false impression of myself."

"Even if it were just a few shots?"

"You know, Liza, my life isn't all that exciting. I tend to avoid parties of this sort."

"I'm sure you do. It would be for only a few minutes, though—to heighten interest in your work. Later, we'll see if we should keep the shots or edit them out. Nothing's set in stone. But believe me, working on a David Navarre property is something many people would give their eyeteeth for."

"As far as I'm concerned, he's a client like anyone else."

"Perhaps, but for the American viewer, he presents a certain image of France: cultured but not snobbish, egalitarian, and educated, with a certain *joie de vivre*."

Benjamin almost smirked. Was that the image of French men most Americans were buying these days? How was that for stereotyping?

"Let me just repeat, Mr. Cooker. I'm asking for only a few minutes."

Benjamin sighed. "All right. Just promise you'll be quick and discreet."

"You have my word. A few shots, and then we're done. And thank you. The party will give our project a touch of glamour."

"I hope you're right, Ms. Stechelmann, but I fear you'll wind up bored to tears."

3

As the sun sank behind a thick curtain of poplars, Château de Pray was coming to life. The clatter of pots and pans in the kitchen was rising to the rooms on the second floor. Frederic Brisset was busy presiding over the sous chefs and others preparing the evening meal.

After unpacking and lingering under scalding showers, Benjamin and Virgile joined the film crew waiting patiently in the lobby. Freshly shaved and smelling of cologne, the two men from Bordeaux had selected outfits in keeping with their personal preferences and the nature of the gathering.

"You don't think we look like country bumpkins, boss?" Virgile asked, adjusting the collar of his fitted jacket. He had slipped it on over a light cashmere sweater, perfect for the unreliable spring weather.

Benjamin gave his assistant a once-over. The winemaker preferred more classic clothes for himself, but Virgile was no slouch when it came to attire. "I don't know what you're talking about. Why are you fretting, Virgile?"

"I don't know. I have the feeling we smell like hay."

Benjamin chuckled. "We're from Bordeaux, son. How could we possibly smell like hay? And even if we did, what would be so wrong with that? We're also men of the vine. 'In the spring, at the end of the day, you should smell like dirt.'"

"Is that a quote, boss?"

"Yes: Margaret Atwood."

"It's just that I'm not in the habit of hanging out with movers and shakers from Paris."

"The crowd probably will be a bit... What's the word? A bit show-biz."

"Don't get me wrong. I'm looking forward to this get-together. But I'm nervous, too."

Benjamin patted his assistant's shoulder. "Virgile, you've had the opportunity to meet some very influential and highly regarded people since coming to work for me. You'll handle any celebrities we meet tonight. Just wear that smile of yours. I've seen how it wins people over. Promise me, though, that you won't use it to charm any starlets. According to our director, we've got an early morning."

Virgile grinned. "Okay, boss."

They climbed into Benjamin's Mercedes. Despite the nip in the air, they had taken the top down at Liza Stechelmann's request. She wanted to film them in the golden light of the sunset. The film truck was a few meters behind, with Fabrice leaning perilously out the passenger-side door to capture the picturesque image of the two winemakers.

"Off to a good start," Benjamin grumbled, chafing at the unwanted attention this was bound to get them. That Liza had asked him to drive more slowly than he wanted only made it worse.

Highway 751 moseyed along the slumbering waters of the Loire River. After passing Montlouis, they crossed over the river and drove through the village of Vouvray, with its slate-topped roofs. They passed the Petit Côteau estate below Château Moncontour and continued on the winding road of the Vallée Coquette. The tufa houses were tinged orange under the last rays of the sun.

Without signaling, Benjamin turned into a pebble drive, where a wooden sign with italic lettering read "Château de Tremblay." He waited for Liza and her assistants, knowing they'd be eager to capture the moment of arrival at David Navarre's estate.

Sure enough, the cameraman was still hanging out the door as they made their way toward the château. "You'd think they'd be a little more discreet," Benjamin muttered.

Virgile looked at his side mirror. "That guy Fabrice must have some phenomenal abs to be leaning out that way and still hanging onto his camera."

Closer to the château, dozens of luxury cars were lined up in a small field. Two helicopters surrounded by uniformed guards were perched on a nearby landing pad.

Virgile let out a whistle. "Some estate, huh."

"You can say that again. It explains some of David's dubious career choices."

The château stood on a solid foundation dating from the twelfth century. A Renaissance restyling hadn't diminished the mansion's robust beginnings. The corner towers still had their steep conical roofs, and carved corbels set off the mullioned windows with panels of pastel-colored stained glass.

A sizable vineyard maintained like an English garden surrounded the château. There was no trace of a pretentious lawn, stylized bushes, or flowerbeds. Here the vineyards reigned. Rows of vines stretched as far as the eye could see, floating on the horizon of the Vouvray plateau.

"It must cost an arm and a leg to maintain this place," Virgile said.

"He's accepted roles that are beneath him just to keep it going."

"Now I understand why he makes so many movies. At his age, staying in leading-man shape can't be easy."

"No, it's not. Before every film, he goes on a strict diet and quits drinking. He keeps up this regimen until he's on set again. David Navarre's a man who does nothing half way. Take all this." Benjamin swept his arm across the vineyard. "He dived into the wine business with passion, and unlike some other people, he doesn't pretend to know everything. He's actually rather sharp, and with time, he's become more discerning. For this estate alone, he's committed enormous amounts of money to cellar renovations and new plantings. And what you see is just part of his holdings. He just bought acreage in Napa Valley, and he's invested in Côtes de Blaye and Saint-Émilion. He also has properties in Saint-Nicolas-de-Bourgueil. And then, of course, there's the parcel he wants us to look at."

"He's crazy to be spending every euro he makes on expanding his vines, when he doesn't know how long he'll land the big roles."

"That's exactly why I like him," Benjamin said, smiling.

"Because he's crazy?"

"No, Virgile, because he's committed." Benjamin climbed out of the convertible and smoothed his light-blue linen jacket.

"Please, try not to stand out," he said to Liza, who had jumped from her van with both feet. "David gave me his permission over the phone, but I'm counting on you to follow us without…"

She stopped him. "Don't worry about a thing. You'll hardly notice us."

The two technicians kept their distance as Benjamin and Virgile made their way to the courtyard. Torch lamps glowed in the twilight, and the walls seemed to sway gently in the light of the flames.

Benjamin picked up the humming of conversation inside the château, interspersed with peals of laughter. He took a breath and opened the door, pretending he didn't have a four-person entourage on his heels.

4

The winemaker found himself caught up in an animated crowd of heavy-hitters and wannabes. He elbowed his way through the horde in front of a copious buffet, where the estate wine was flowing like water.

Virgile was wide-eyed. "Boss, I think that's Max Armond, the director. And isn't the other guy the former soccer star who hosts *La France a un incroyable talent?*"

"I recognize them, son," Benjamin answered. "I caught Armond's last film, but I don't watch much TV."

He took in the crowd. Show business types were rubbing shoulders with anonymous characters who were clearly filthy rich, despite their casual outfits. A bearded man in a biker jacket and jeans had cornered a twentyish blond woman in a low-cut sequined dress. She was using her full wine glass to keep him at bay. Strutting near a second buffet was a baby-faced lawyer with long hair. Benjamin knew who he was: a specialist in lost causes and scandalous cases, an intelligent and obscene braggart who was often in the news. Nearby, an aging rock performer pursued by the tax authorities sported piercings as ostentatious as his music. The winemaker watched as he made his way toward a hip young author whose image Benjamin had seen on a new release at the bookstores. The author was surrounded by a group of good-looking women, and the old rocker no doubt wanted in on the action.

Benjamin took Virgile's elbow. "It's stuffy in here. Let's go into the lounge. It won't be as loud and suffocating."

"Can't say I'd mind doing that, boss, although I am intrigued. See that guy over there?" Virgile lifted his chin to point out a man in a body-hugging Sutton suit. "He's one of the top plastic surgeons in Paris. I've read stories about him. He knows exactly how many botulinum toxin injections every person in this crowd has had. He's filthy rich—does eyes, noses, breasts. He even rejuvenates the private parts, if you catch my drift."

"That's enough, Virgile. Some things I don't need to know."

"I'll spare you the details. But these people don't come by their gorgeous looks naturally."

"I sense you're feeling your Bergerac roots, son."

"I admit it. These aren't the people I'd hang out with even if I were rich."

"You're not alone on that score, although there are a few people here whom I can call my friends." Benjamin looked over at the buffet table. "I think I'll see what they have to eat."

Murmuring "excuse me" several times, he squeezed past twenty or so people and helped himself to several *petits fours*. On his way back, he caught sight of a silver tray with glasses of red wine. A server held out a stemmed glass, but just as Benjamin took it, someone bumped his elbow. The wine went flying into the server's pristine white shirt, leaving a fist-sized stain just above his waist.

"*Merde!*" the server cursed.

Before Benjamin could offer to find a bottle of club soda or even apologize, the young man glared at him and walked away.

"Maybe this party was a bad idea," Benjamin muttered. But his mood lifted a few seconds later, when he spotted Virgile. His assistant had matured over the years, from the boy fresh out of school to

the more sophisticated but still good-hearted—
and, yes, charming—young man he was now. True,
Virgile had always been prone to falling into bed
with beautiful women, and this had made Benjamin stubbornly opposed to a serious relationship
with his daughter, Margaux, for whom he suspected Virgile still carried a torch. Sometimes he sensed
that Virgile had cut back on his liaisons, but he
would never broach the subject. "Maybe someday…" Benjamin thought before rejecting the notion altogether.

The winemaker was so occupied with dis-
missing the idea of a Margaux-Virgile match
that he nearly walked into two men who were in
the midst of a heated conversation. He had met
both of them at a reception in Paris hosted by his
publisher. Jean-Paul Gayraud was a high-profile
producer, and American expat Lee Friedman was
a screenwriter who worked on productions in
both the United States and France.

Friedman had consulted with the winemaker a
few months after the Paris reception, when he was
working on the script for a film set in Bordeaux,
and even though the screenwriter's cynicism sometimes annoyed Benjamin, the two men had formed
a casual friendship.

Despite the blaring techno music, Benjamin could make out that the two men were quarreling over one of the screenwriter's projects.

Seeing the winemaker, Lee stopped arguing and grinned. "Well, well! Look who's here—the esteemed creator of *The Cooker Guide,* the unassailable authority on French wines! Jean-Paul, do you have any idea how many books this man has sold?"

"I didn't mean to interrupt your conversation," Benjamin said before Gayraud could answer. "I can see you're discussing an important matter."

"Always the gentleman," Lee said.

Benjamin, taken aback by the tone, was tempted to move along, but instead, he looked around for a table where he could set his food. Finding one, he motioned to Virgile to join them.

"Actually, I'm glad we ran into each other," Lee said. "Jean-Paul and I were just talking about my latest project, which he green-lighted six months ago."

The winemaker raised an eyebrow. "Oh? Tell me about it."

"I think it would interest you, Benjamin. It's an adaptation of a highly acclaimed crime caper, *The Vineyard Plot.* You may have read it."

Of course Benjamin had read it. Stephen Burrows, the main character, was a well-known food and wine critic. Burrows was loosely based on Benjamin himself. The fictional food critic-turned-sleuth had solved a double homicide in Normandy while nibbling Camembert and sipping Calvados.

Benjamin's publisher had given him a heads-up as soon as the first draft crossed his desk. "I want you to read the draft before we even touch it. I won't publish this book without your imprimatur," he had said.

Benjamin had gone through the *The Vineyard Plot* and thoroughly enjoyed it. In fact, he was a bit flattered.

"It seems my project has hit a snag since Gayraud here gave his okay," Lee said, looking straight at the producer. "I've yet to see my contract. I was asking him what I could do to free things up."

Benjamin wasn't surprised. The sixtyish Jean-Paul Gayraud was one of the most powerful producers in Paris, but also one of the stingiest. He was likable enough, although Benjamin had never cared to be his friend. With a slight build, tinted spectacles and graying hair, he had the look of an affable predator.

"I'm sure we'll be able to resolve the problem," Gayraud said, his forced smile revealing his crooked teeth. He turned to Benjamin. "We must get together again to discuss that documentary. You're still in favor of doing it, right?"

"Not just in favor. Enthusiastic, especially now that we're filming."

Benjamin had said this with no hint of hostility. Negotiations with Gayraud had taken place a year earlier for a documentary on the Bordeaux winemaker's prestigious career. But the financial arrangements hit a snag when Gayraud failed to secure backing from any foreign television networks. The producer balked at advancing his own money, and once it became evident that he would have to assume all the risk, he dropped the ball without the courtesy of a letter or phone call. Benjamin wasn't used to such rude treatment.

Gayraud, obviously surprised, mustered a smile. "So someone else is doing the documentary? I'm pleased for you, Benjamin! Truly pleased. Who's in charge of the project?"

Benjamin waved his hand evasively. He wasn't about to go there. "Good people, very good people, as a matter of fact," he said simply.

"How lucky for you," Lee said, looking disgusted. "I wish I could say the same for my project."

"As I said, Lee, I think we can resolve the problem with a bit of patience."

"Patience?" Lee responded, his voice booming over the noise. "How long must a patient man wait?"

Heads turned in their direction, and Benjamin feared Lee would say something he'd regret. The screenwriter's scathing putdowns were legend. He was relieved when David Navarre's arrival cut his friend short.

"Ah, the man of the hour!" Benjamin said a little too cheerfully.

The actor delivered a hard slap to the producer's back. "So, you crook, still at it?"

"Just a friendly conversation," Gayraud said, pale-faced.

"You'd better get a move on. Your deal with this fellow shouldn't be dragging on this way."

When David spoke, those around him dropped their guard. He put people at ease. It was in his relaxed posture, his saunter, and his bad-boy smile. Benjamin, who studied people almost as carefully as he studied wines, understood the look was intentional. There was much more to his actor-friend, and Benjamin was one of David's few associates who knew how driven he was—driven to maintain his place in the movie industry, driven to succeed in the wine business, and driven to stay youthful. Unfortunately, David also drank too much, and if he didn't maintain his discipline, it would be his undoing.

He turned to Benjamin. "I'm happy you came. We must get together tomorrow to go over my plans for that parcel."

Gayraud tried to ingratiate himself. "Just like you, David: the star of French cinema collaborating with the star of French winemaking."

"I don't give a damn about Benjamin's place in the celebrity galaxy, Gayraud. I asked him to help me because he's the best."

"And you're one person who's willing to pay for the best," Lee said, "unlike other people, whose euros have to be pried from their clutches. Right, Jean-Paul?" Lee was still itching for a fight. His smile was nasty, and his eyebrow was raised.

The producer lowered his gaze, acquiescing to the screenwriter. A moment later he cleared his throat and looked toward the doorway. "Gentlemen, I must say goodnight, as I have an early morning." Gayraud took his leave. Benjamin, Lee,

Virgile, and David followed him with their eyes until he disappeared in the crowd.

"'The devil lies brooding in the miser's chest.'" It was Lee.

Alarmed, Benjamin turned to his screenwriter friend, whose nasty smile turned benign. Lee winked at the winemaker. "You see, Benjamin, even an American expat can quote the likes of your countryman Thomas Fuller.

5

Virgile had tired of the conversation. He drained his glass of Champagne and set it down on the table, next to the winemaker's plate.

He gave his companions a nod and walked away, returning to the reception hall, where people seemed to be having more fun. A disk jockey with rose-colored glasses, a skin-tight leatherette T-shirt, and safety pins piercing his upper lip was beat matching on vinyl. Several bleached and natural blondes were dancing, their arms raised and their hips swaying. The heavy synchronized thumping struck Virgile right in the chest. He snatched another glass, gulped the contents, and put it back on the server's tray. The lithe young man with slicked-back hair, mustache, and a wine stain on his shirt paid him no mind, preoccupied as he was with keeping his glasses upright while snaking between the dancers.

"Are you lost?"

Virgile froze. There was something familiar about the voice: slightly fluted, both soft and husky. He glanced over his shoulder and was petrified. He had seen her in magazine and television images—languishing on a yacht in the Bay of Antibes, climbing the palace stairs at Cannes, displaying her duplex near the wealthy Parisian Trocadéro neighborhood, holding up a César, a tear of joy clinging to her eyelashes, laughing at a private party in Bains-Douches. Simone Margerolle was a fantasy woman who existed in a vague, distant place. And there she was, in flesh and blood. More in the flesh, as it were: curvaceous breasts beneath the shimmering silk fabric of her plum-colored sheath, voluptuous hips, and tiny waist.

Virgile forced himself to focus on her intense blue eyes.

"Shush! Don't say a word," she said, putting a finger on his lips.

Virgile picked up the scent of pears. She'd dipped her finger in Champagne. He had no choice but to comply. He was tongue-tied.

"Let me guess. Film? Theater? Modeling?"

He worked to dispel the mental image of this gorgeous actress licking the Champagne off her finger. "Nothing like acting or modeling," he finally said.

"Literature? Visual arts?" She looked up at him, smiling flirtatiously, aware, he knew, of the effect she was having.

At this, Virgile began to relax. Flirting was something he knew how to do. He mustered a coy look. "You're getting colder."

Simone wrinkled her nose. "I hope you're not in public relations, like everyone else."

"I'm not like everyone else."

Simone tilted her head. "Hmm, the plot thickens, I love that! An athlete, then?"

"In my spare time."

"Don't tell me you're a gigolo!"

Virgile smiled. "Would that be so terrible?"

"You do have what it takes, I'd say," Simone said, sizing him up. "You've never considered taking advantage of your killer physique?"

"Taking advantage?"

"What I mean is, you could use it to live on. There's no shame in that."

"No shame, I grant you. But I'll leave that to other people. It's not my thing."

"Come now, be nice. Tell me who's hiding behind that charming face. I've never seen you at the château before."

Virgile looked around the room. "It's my first time here. Nice place."

"You mean gorgeous... Elegant... Over the top but still classy. Like everything else related to David. So, are you going to tell me why you're at this party? Or is it shameful?"

Virgile sighed. "Sorry to disappoint you, but I'm no celebrity or VIP. I'm the assistant to Benjamin Cooker, the winemaker who's working with Mr. Navarre on the vineyard he wants to revive." He held his breath, waiting for Simone to murmur "that's nice" and move on.

But she didn't. "I've heard a lot about your Benjamin Cooker," she said. "David swears by him. Now I understand. That explains the adorable accent from the southwest of France. Are you from Bordeaux?"

"At present, yes. But I'm originally from Bergerac—Montravel, to be exact."

"I'm not familiar with Montravel, but it doesn't matter. Will you take me out on the dance floor? I love this number."

"I'm a very bad dancer."

"So what? Make believe you're good. And make me happy."

Simone took Virgile's hand and led him to an empty spot on the crowded dance floor. He step-tapped as best he could, out of kilter, a little drunk. The Champagne was making him dizzy, and pleasantly so. Simone swayed gracefully, brushing against him.

Virgile couldn't quite believe what was happening. It wasn't that he had never been with a stunning woman. He was experienced. But this was different—an otherworldly flirtation that put him off-balance. She wrapped her arm around his waist and rested her head on his shoulder. It wasn't the hand-in-glove sensation he'd felt with Margaux. The fit wasn't quite right. Still, he felt himself surrender. Her neck smelled of vanilla and alcohol. Her skin was moist. He stroked her back. Her breasts pressed against his chest felt unbelievably delicious.

They danced a long while, both close and apart, depending on the music. Now and then a friend of the actress would come up and whisper something in her ear, and she would burst out laughing, throwing her head back and showing her perfect white teeth. She clung to Virgile tighter and tighter and murmured a few words. She needed Champagne, more Champagne, and still more. He complied and rushed over to the bar. But when he returned to the dance floor, Simone had disappeared.

He wandered for a good hour, looking through all the rooms with a glass in each hand. He went outside to scan the shadows in the courtyard, passed the buffet tables again and again, and waited in vain near the bathroom while sipping from one of the glasses. The actress was nowhere to be found.

He had downed the second glass when he ran into Benjamin, whose tired face betrayed his irritation.

"What have you been doing, Virgile? I've been looking for you."

Virgile decided to keep the encounter with Simone Margerolle to himself. "I was just dancing, boss."

"And did you exchange phone numbers with any of the lovelies you danced with? Oh, I for-got—isn't Instagram the way you young people stay in touch these days?"

Virgile gave Benjamin a curious look. "How did you know about Instagram, boss?"

"Give me some credit, would you? I do read, you know. But so much for social media. We need to take off. We have a lot of work to do tomorrow, and it's already late."

Virgile surveyed the scene and realized many of the partygoers had left. Several of the drunken ones who remained were sprawled on the banquettes. The proudest had lost all dignity, while those who didn't care were just being themselves. The photographer from the magazine *Voici!* was snapping pictures that he knew would be unprintable but would come in handy for his personal files. No one seemed to mind.

"When did Liza and her assistants leave?" Virgile asked.

"Actually, not too long ago. They finished filming, and, surprisingly, David told them they could stay. As long as they were inconspicuous, I didn't mind."

"So where's David? I'd like to say goodnight."

"I haven't seen him. He was drinking heavily. He probably went off to bed."

The disc jockey was packing his equipment, and the catering crew was picking up the dishes and glasses. Just as Benjamin and Virgile were opening the door to leave, a cry rang out, silencing the clatter of porcelain and crystal.

"Simone is dead!"

6

An eerie blue pall hung over the room as Benjamin drank his tea and watched the news. The winemaker hadn't gotten to bed until well past two in the morning, and then he had tossed and turned, unable to still his restless legs. Finally giving up shortly after five, he showered, dressed, placed his breakfast order, and waited for the sunlight to start streaming through the French doors leading to his small balcony. Still, when he turned on the television, he wondered if he had conjured up what had happened at Château de Tremblay.

The young actress Simone Margerolle was clinging to life at a hospital in Tours, having been found unconscious in the wine cellar of famed actor David Navarre. The hospital director in Tours said she was in a deep coma. A thumbnail picture in the lower-left corner of the screen displayed the smiling actress beside her lover, whose neatly trimmed salt-and-pepper hair underscored their age difference. The photograph had been taken a few weeks earlier, during filming of the new Max Armond movie. Benjamin couldn't miss the glazed look in David's eyes or the flushed cheeks, which his voguish white stubble couldn't mask.

Benjamin sighed and took a bite of his toast with marmalade. He looked back at the television and saw that a young meteorologist in form-fitting jeans and a shirt with no tie had replaced the reporter. His tone was borderline playful, which annoyed the winemaker. A high-pressure system was settling over the country. There was nothing else to report, aside from some scattered showers on the Aquitaine coast.

A commercial, a short segment on humanitarian aid in Mali, and a commentary on the surprising benefits of artichokes followed the weather. Then there was an interview with an Emmanuel Macron spokesman, who touted modest gains in business confidence and job growth. The polite banter suggested that France might awaken in a good mood. But it couldn't offset the depressing news about Simone Margerolle. Benjamin was in a morose frame of mind as he rewound the events.

A member of the catering staff had been carting unopened bottles to the Château de

Tremblay wine cellar when he found Simone lying on the cold stone floor, presumably dead. The staff member's screams had roused the few remaining drunken guests. Benjamin and Virgile had rushed to the cellar entrance. A security guard, however, had gotten there already and was barring the door. The guard had herded everyone into the library and instructed them to wait. To Benjamin's relief, he returned a few moments later and announced that Simone was still alive. An ambulance would arrive soon.

At this point David's personal assistant had gotten up and slipped out of the library. She came back several minutes later and pulled Benjamin aside.

"Mr. Cooker, I don't know what to do," she whispered. "I tried to wake Mr. Navarre, but I couldn't get him up. He just spoke some gibberish and went back to sleep."

"He drank too much," Benjamin answered, shaking his head. "Just let him rest. The security guard seems to be handling everything, and there's nothing David can do for Simone right now. Besides, the police will be here with a barrage of questions in the morning. He'll need his wits about him."

The personal assistant had agreed. She found an armchair near the fireplace and started scrolling through her smartphone.

When the ambulance finally arrived, Benjamin watched as two paramedics rushed toward the cellar entrance and down the stairs. He could hear them working in tandem to stabilize Simone and get her on the gurney. She was as white as the sheet covering her body when they came back upstairs. Benjamin glanced at Virgile. He couldn't miss the concern on his assistant's face.

The paramedics wheeled the gurney outside and raced off in the ambulance, its blue lights flashing.

As soon as the security guard allowed them to leave, Benjamin and Virgile had returned to the hotel and crawled into their respective beds.

Finishing his toast, Benjamin wiped his mouth and turned off the television. "Come in," he said, looking toward the door before Virgile even knocked.

Trailing his latest scent, a woodsy-citrus blend, Virgile entered the room. "How did you know I was out there, boss?"

"How did I know? I could smell you from the hallway!"

§ § §

Virgile could see the winemaker was in a foul mood. It wasn't that he didn't understand. He wasn't feeling so great himself. Simone Margerolle, the beautiful actress who had vanished on him the previous night, was in critical condition at the Tours hospital. But he didn't want to make matters worse by irritating his boss. He stepped into the bathroom and washed his face and neck to minimize the smell of the cologne.

"Better?" he asked as he came out, drying his hands. He put the towel down and took a chair near the winemaker.

Benjamin ignored him and took another sip of his tea.

"Liza Stechelmann is waiting for us in the courtyard."

"Oh," Benjamin said, putting his cup down and finally making eye contact. "I had forgotten about her."

"She'd like to get an early start. It seems the morning light is excellent for getting shots."

"So what? The right light's her problem, not mine."

Virgile didn't respond.

"And when it rains? What does she do with herself then? Quit working?"

Virgile changed the subject. "What's the program for today?"

"Pinon."

"I'm not following, boss."

"Pinon! Doesn't that mean anything to you?"

"Um, I'm afraid I don't understand."

"François Pinon! Fifteen hectares of chenin in the Vallée de Cousse!"

"Of course. Considering how long I've been hearing about him, I can't be forgiven. That said, I've only tasted his Vouvray Trois Argiles."

Benjamin paused and finished his tea. Then he looked back at Virgile with an expression that verged on pleasant. "I remember. It was two years ago in Bordeaux. We were at the lab, and I was confirming my notes for the *Wine Spectator:* 'Ebullient, with ripe fruit, refreshing acidity, and Vouvray's characteristic chalky minerality. An ideal springtime wine.' If we're lucky, François will part with a bottle or two when we see him today."

"You've got quite a memory, boss."

"And you'd do well to follow my example," Benjamin said, pointing to his forehead. "Everything must be stored in here. Classified, archived, recorded. Every aroma, every vintage, everything, you understand? Once it's in your head you must never let it out."

"But, boss, what about the little notebook you keep tucked in your jacket? You scribble in that all the time."

"That's backup, son. The brain is your primary information-storage system."

"If you say so. But can we go easy on our brains today? My head's aching. I had a hard time sleeping after we got back here."

"I didn't sleep well either. Then I turned on the news. How is it we always fall feet first into this type of thing?"

"Maybe we have a knack for attracting trouble."

"But this is a bit much! We've come to Touraine for a nice little visit. Of course, we've been retained to do some work, but it promised to be a week of pleasure, tasting wines and staying in a dream hotel with an outstanding chef. What could be better? Just what we've needed to pause and recharge, right? Then wham! A young woman is found near death in our client's wine cellar."

"And not just any woman," murmured Virgile.

"Apparently she's a talented actress. But since I don't have time for more than one or two movies a year, I wouldn't recognize her in person. I understand she's rather pretty."

"More like a bombshell!" Virgile blurted.

"What do you mean? Explosive? Volatile?"

"In a way…"

"What's going on, son? I saw that look on your face when they were taking her out to the ambulance. You didn't happen to meet her at the party, did you?"

"Sort of," Virgile stammered. "That is, it was strange…"

"Strange? Tell me more."

Virgile felt the blood rushing to his face. He didn't want to reveal too much. "We talked briefly, and then we danced. That was it. Voilà!"

"Nothing else?"

"There were a lot of people. I lost her in the crowd."

"But it seems you saw enough of her to be shook up."

"She's not the kind of woman you walk away from feeling like you're still in one piece."

"Meanwhile, we don't know whether she herself will come out of this in one piece. Nor do we know what happened to her."

"It's what everyone in the dining room was talking about when I was having breakfast. Liza and her assistants arrived while I was there."

"And Liza and her assistants? What do they think?"

"Fabrice and Hugo weren't saying much. Liza and I talked a little. She's shaken. She's more sensitive than she looks."

"Sensitive or not, she seems to be a woman of her word. She said they'd be almost inconspicuous, and I hardly noticed them once we were at the château."

"Really, boss, Liza's a nice woman. Sensible, no nonsense. Besides, if I might make a comment…"

"Go right ahead."

"Well, okay, I think you've been a bit rude. There's no reason to be so off-putting, especially since she's tried to accommodate you." Virgile cringed, ready for a reprimand. But the winemaker surprised him.

"You think I've been inappropriate?"

"Honestly, it's come close. She could be offended."

Benjamin sighed and got up. "You're right, son. You're a trusting soul. I could learn from you. But remember this: 'Trust is the easiest thing in the world to lose and the hardest thing in the world to get back.' That's R.J. Williams, the Australian bootmaker."

"But boss, you wear Lobbs."

Benjamin put his hand on Virgile's shoulder. "Like John Lobb, Williams was a native of Cornwall."

7

Finally rid of his glum mood, Benjamin once again took down the top of his convertible. He wanted to breathe the spring air and feel the warmth of the sun on his neck. He planned to take advantage of the drive to François Pinon's estate to prepare Virgile, always his student, for the visit.

"I'm sure you know that for centuries the Loire Valley has been the stamping ground for royals, writers such as Honoré de Balzac and François Rabelais, and more than a few celebrities, David Navarre included. It's known as France's garden. The list of famous châteaus is endless: Chenonceau, Chambord, Amboise, Cheverny, Blois, Langeais…"

Virgile nodded while reaching into a pocket for his sunglasses. "Yeah, boss. Mick Jagger owns Château la Fourchette in Indre-et-Loire, a few kilometers from Amboise. When he was a kid, he camped in the Loire Valley with his parents, and he was so attached to the area, he bought the château in nineteen eighty. He plays cricket with the local team, and you can spot him on occasion at the local pizzeria."

"I can see you're keeping up with all your pop stars, Virgile."

"Boss, Mick Jagger's not exactly one of my pop stars. He's older than you."

Benjamin laughed. "Thank you, Virgile. For once you've made me feel young."

"No problem."

"At any rate, I'm eager to find out what François Pinon has for us today. His Vouvrays are classic and soulful. The younger generation of growers is getting the attention these days, Virgile, but you won't find a more consistent and dependable grower. François's Vouvrays are exquisite. And by the way, there's no place on earth that can match the Loire Valley's chenin grape. This is its ancestral home."

"Kind of like all the royalty that used to live around here."

"Yes, son, kind of like that." Benjamin glanced at his assistant. Virgile appeared to be drinking it all in, so he continued. "Vouvray's one of the most diverse wines you'll ever come across—ranging from dry to sweet and still to sparkling—but they're all prized for their intrinsic nature. Despite everything I've written about Vouvray in my *Cooker Guide*, I can't top the *Wine Folly's* description: it's 'loved for its delicate floral aromas and boisterous taste that will pucker your lips and make you immediately wish for another sip.'"

"Sounds romantic. One sip, and you're smitten. Love at first sight."

"I wouldn't say they're the same thing. I think smitten is more superficial than love." Benjamin crested a hill and passed a slow-moving car. He felt Virgile's eyes on him and glanced his way. "What is it, son?"

"Can I ask a question, boss?"

"Go ahead."

"Was that how it was with you and Mrs. Cooker? Love at first sight?"

Benjamin shifted in his seat. He had never been asked this before. Had it been anyone else, he wouldn't have answered, but because it was Virgile, he did. "Yes, you could say that, although I wouldn't use those exact words. I had many liaisons in my youth, like you, but when I met Elisabeth, that was it for me. She had grace, intelligence, and heart. She was quick and witty too. In all these years, I've never been bored, and every time I pull into the drive at Grangebelle, I'm excited to see her. What about you, son? Do you believe in love at first sight?"

"I do, boss." Virgile fell silent, and Benjamin waited, sensing his unease. "But it hurts like hell when you believe the person you love isn't in sync with you. It can make you do things."

"Just what kind of things, son?"

Virgile looked out the window. "Oh, I don't know. Like succumbing to someone else who finds you appealing."

"Hmm, so you're saying that if you can't have the Vouvray, you'd allow yourself to be charmed by an Anjou?"

Benjamin didn't give Virgile time to respond. He had almost missed the entrance to the Pinon estate, which had no ostentatious gates or billboards touting the owner's wine. "Why don't we take this up later," he said, relieved to drop the subject, as it was too personal for his taste.

François Pinon's home was modest, simple, and inviting, a reflection of its owner. François welcomed everyone who came to sample the fruit of his labor with an open mind. Benjamin and Virgile were no exception, and the winemaker appreciated this. All too often, vintners and brokers put on airs or fawned over him. It was a pleasure to spend time here.

Benjamin introduced the members of the documentary team, and François, in a cap and plaid shirt, showed the winemaker and his assistant to a wooden table outside the old vinification cellar, with its wall of paned windows. He excused himself for a moment and went into his house, which was adjacent to the cellar.

Liza issued instructions, and she and her team got busy making themselves as inconspicuous as they had at the party. Fabrice and Hugo found crouching spots near the house. Fabrice had the grace of a cat, despite his muscular build. Hugo, who wasn't as fit, wobbled slightly as he unpacked his sound equipment. Liza had turned off her cell phone and was scanning the vineyards for bucolic images.

The winemaker was taking in the earthy smells when François emerged with a loaf of bread and a jar of rillettes.

"You spoil us, François." Benjamin said, already salivating. "Virgile, rillettes were a Pinon family specialty at one time. Now he buys a whole hog and brings in the local charcutier to have the rillettes made to his specification. They're wonderful. The store-bought variety is much too fatty."

Having set out the food, François went into the vinification cellar and returned with a wire basket containing six bottles.

The unusual career path of this solid and demanding man, with a serious face softened by a beard had impressed Benjamin so much, he had devoted an entire page to him in the first edition of his *Cooker Guide*. François, the descendent of several generations of Touraine farmers and vintners, had abandoned rural life to attend the prestigious École Normale. After a brief stint as a professor, he continued his studies and became a child psychologist. For a time, he worked beside the French pediatrician and psychoanalyst Françoise Dolto. When his parents retired, however, the call of his native land proved irresistible. He left Paris and took up the torch. The city dweller found he had forgotten nothing about working the land, and he still had the passion for it. François gradually abandoned mixed farming, and the estate had since become emblematic of the Vouvray appellation.

François appeared to be oblivious to the film crew as he explained his work. Benjamin listened attentively, even though he was versed in the methods: the pruning, scraping, sucker removal, harvesting, plowing, spraying, splicing, trimming, sorting, clarifying, racking, filtering, and other day-to-day and often exhausting routines of this conscientious winemaker. Now and then Benjamin broke in with a technical question, but he was eager to taste the wines. François obliged by filling their stem glasses.

"As you know, we had that disastrous hail storm in 2012 and very small yields in 2013, but we recovered nicely," François said. "What I'm pouring now is the first Les Déronnières that I bottled."

Benjamin studied the color and sniffed. Finally, he chewed, taking out his notebook a few minutes later, unscrewing the cap of his fountain pen, and making his notations in quick, tight writing.

"2014 Vouvray Déronnières: Cuvée grown on hilltop above Pinon cave. 18 grams per liter residual sugar, 12.4 percent alcohol and strong acidity. Similar to demi-sec, but with fantastic minerality and balance. Subtle aromas of dried pear, lemon, and gravel. Minerality and saline on the palate, with white fruit, lemon, and herbal notes."

He put his pen down and didn't say anything. Finally, he looked at his host. "A simply stunning wine, François. Elegant and complex. It should age beautifully."

François smiled and poured a second vintage. Once again, Benjamin studied, sniffed, chewed, and picked up his pen: "2014 Vouvray Silex Noir: From clay parcels over limestone with black flint. Unique mineral character. Nicely balanced, with 12.1 percent alcohol and 15 grams residual sugars. Complex aromas of citrus, floral, dried pear, and licorice. Concentrated palate of white fruits, minerals, and citrus. Delicious and likely to improve when aged a dozen years or longer."

Benjamin turned to Virgile, eager to hear his thoughts.

"Bright and expressive," Virgile said. "But at the same time, precise."

The winemaker nodded.

"Now we'll go back a few years," François said, filling fresh glasses. "This is our Premiere Trie Vouvray, 2003, at its peak."

Benjamin admired the lovely color and followed the ritual. "Golden robe with amber sheen," he wrote. "Wisteria and pear and poached peach on the nose, with a touch of praline. Honeysuckle notes with no cloying sweetness. A refined wine."

He jotted one more sentence before putting his notebook and fountain pen back in his pocket. "Would you mind sending samples to a journalist friend of mine?" he asked François.

Benjamin's friend was familiar with this type of varietal, and he wanted her opinion. The winemaker wasn't afraid to express his thoughts, but he was also receptive to the opinions of esteemed colleagues. When he needed to have his judgments confirmed or contradicted, he didn't hesitate to consult with trusted wine experts whose tasting notes he found relevant.

François said he'd get the samples off right away, and Benjamin relaxed. The tasting session continued under the pale spring sunlight, and no one had any desire to leave. Before packing up, Liza asked Fabrice to film the inside of the vinification cellar, along with the limestone caverns.

An hour later, Benjamin, a little tipsy, reluctantly decided it was time to go. But he agreed to taste one more glass that François insisted on pouring. He admired the fine bubbles and the aroma of small dried fruit.

After promising to return in the autumn to grill sausages on the fireplace and taste the first juices of the harvest, Benjamin and Virgile said their good-byes and headed toward the Mercedes.

"Here, you drive," Benjamin said, handing Virgile his keys. "Let's go back to the hotel. I was thinking we should check on David, but we can do that tomorrow. Considering all the wine we've drunk with no spitting and the restless night, I could use a nap."

"No problem, boss. You get some shut eye. While you're sleeping, there's something I need to do."

Benjamin leaned against the seat and closed his eyes. He didn't bother to ask.

8

Virgile pulled into the Château de Pray parking lot and turned off the engine. Benjamin roused himself and opened the passenger-side door. Virgile stopped him before he could step out.

"Ah, boss, could I borrow your car for a bit?"

"Why do you need the car, son?"

"I have to run an errand."

"What kind of errand?" Benjamin was beginning to look annoyed.

Virgile had come up with a reason as soon as Benjamin handed him the car keys. "I know you won't think it's important, boss, but I forgot my hair gel."

Now Benjamin was clearly annoyed. "A special trip for hair gel? What is it with you young men? Special gels, cleansers, a hydrating this, a soothing that. What happened to soap and water and a decent haircut like mine?"

"You're right, boss. I should give it some thought."

Benjamin sighed. "All right, son. Take the car. Get your hair gel or whatever. I'm going inside now to take my nap."

Pleased to have gotten that out of the way, Virgile sped out of the parking lot and drove to Tours. He pulled out his cell phone to call the hospital for Simone's room number, but he thought better of it. He was unfamiliar with the privacy policy and didn't want to deal with uninvited questions. Arriving at the hospital, he walked nonchalantly past the visitors' desk and security guards. He found an out-of-the-way directory and located the intensive-care unit. It was on the second floor. Virgile opened the door to the stairwell and looked up and down the hall before entering. He barely registered the tall, well-built man in a polo shirt and jeans who was hurrying away in the distance.

Virgile took the stairs two at a time and breathed a sigh of relief when he spotted two visitors being buzzed into the intensive-care unit. Smiling, he slipped in behind them. He circumvented the central nurses' station and poked his head around the curtain of each doorway until he found her.

Virgile's heart sank. She was as still as a corpse and had so many intravenous lines going into her, he didn't have it in him to count them all. Surrounded by machines and IV bags, she looked tiny and frail. Her forearms were already bruised from the needles, and her long blond hair was matted against her head. Virgile stared at her hands, swollen from the fluids they were giving her. He resisted an urge to reach out and stroke her arm to let her know a friend was there. He was afraid of hurting her.

Virgile looked over at an aide in scrubs, who was scribbling something on a clipboard. He wanted to ask how Simone was doing, but her back was turned. She didn't even acknowledge him when he cleared his throat. A second later, she scurried out of the room.

"Must be busy," he muttered.

No sooner had he pulled a chair over to Simone's bedside than a nurse in similar floral-print scrubs came in, pushing a computer cart. Virgile guessed she was about thirty. This one smiled as she stepped around him to check Simone's IV bags.

"Am I in the way?" he asked, starting to scoot the chair toward the wall.

"Not at all," the nurse answered. "You're fine."

"Fine," Virgile said to himself. "At least some-one is."

He ventured his question. "How's she doing?"

"She's still critical, but she's stable, and that's good."

Virgile didn't want to risk asking about the treatment plan and just nodded.

The nurse walked back to her computer and entered some numbers. "I'm surprised," she said, still looking at the screen. "I thought we'd be mobbed with well-wishers. But you and that other fellow are the only ones who've been up here. Oh yes, a doctor friend of Mr. Navarre's stopped in."

"What about the photographers and reporters?" Virgile asked.

"Oh, the security people would stop anyone with a microphone or camera—at least one they could see. Nope, it's been very quiet."

"You mentioned another fellow?"

"Yeah, a good-looking guy. Tall, well-built, in a polo shirt. He had a man bun. He was here just before you came. I thought maybe he was her boyfriend, but then I remembered she was dating Navarre. They were making a movie around here."

"A muscular guy with a bun, you say." The image of the man in the ground-floor hallway flashed in Virgile's head. "Did you catch his name?"

"No, I've got too much to do to chat much with visitors. He did say he worked behind the scenes in movies or television, I don't remember which."

The nurse said good-bye and wheeled her computer cart out of the room.

"Why was Fabrice here?" he whispered, hoping against hope that Simone would turn her head and answer. As far as Virgile knew, she had never met him. Or had she? Had she danced with Fabrice the same way she'd danced with him? Was the cameraman just as mesmerized? Or was there another reason he'd come to the hospital?

Virgile filed the question away and gazed at the unconscious young woman. She looked so isolated, so alone, and so vulnerable.

Feeling a wave of sympathy, he got up and reached over to smooth her hair. He pushed past his anxiety and took her hand. Maybe she would squeeze his. Nothing happened.

Promising to return, he left the room and walked out of the hospital. He looked around the grounds for signs of news people, maybe even Fabrice. All he saw were hospital workers coming off their shift. He pulled out Benjamin's car key and

drove back to Château de Pray. They were scheduled to spend several more days with Liza, Fabrice,
and Hugo. He'd find out why the brawny cameraman was so interested in Simone Margerolle.

9

Benjamin and Virgile got an early start the next morning to allow for a visit with David Navarre. The two men were quiet as they drove, and the winemaker didn't bother to ask Virgile if he had completed his errand. He was savoring the memory of his tasting with François Pinon when Virgile turned to him.

"It's strange, boss—with all of the region's fancy châteaus and showy history, they hide a lot of their vineyards, kind of like a secret lover."

Benjamin chuckled. "There's no secret. It's all in the geography, son. Here in Vouvray country, the vineyard is often out of sight. But you feel its proximity. I think of it this way: behind the high cliffs pierced with troglodyte caves and beyond the slate roofs, you sense the presence of an army of vines standing guard in rows, ready to confront the assault of rain and biting sun."

"So it's not a lover but, instead, a military division. If you ask me, grape leaves make pretty poor shields." Benjamin ignored Virgile's smirk. His assistant still had a thing or two to learn, and Benjamin had much to impart. He launched into another lecture. "Let me fill you in. With two thousand hectares divided among seven communes, the Vouvray appellation is the true kingdom of chenin, one of the finest and most delicate grape varieties on earth. It can repay a grower a hundred times over if he knows how to take care of it."

Benjamin slowed down to take a curve and then checked on Virgile. He was paying attention. "The Vouvray region lies just east of Tours. It enjoys a rather mild climate. And that's a good thing, because it's not necessarily easy to cultivate this type of vineyard. You must not underestimate the oceanic influence that warms the ground. Autumns are usually sunny, which encourages ripeness and noble rot. That said, the grape can be fickle."

"So we're back to the lover metaphor," Virgile said, grinning.

Benjamin suppressed a scowl. "What I mean by fickle is that the sugar content can determine a year's production. In cool years, production leans toward the drier varieties, including the sparkling Vouvrays. In warmer years, the sweeter Vouvrays tend to dominate."

"To get back to our geography, the vineyards are often on high rises."

"Absolutely—stony plateaus on limestone substrate that loom above the valleys. The white Turonian clay is covered with flinty clay, which gives dry wines their characteristic minerality. And then the calcareous clay gives the sweet wines their well-rounded nature."

"Yes, boss. Turonian. Ninety-four to ninety million years ago, roughly counting. It was the second of six main divisions in the Upper Cretaceous Series."

"I see you still remember something from your days at oenology school."

The winemaker kept going, piling on figures while Virgile listened politely. The region produced about a hundred and fifteen thousand hectoliters of Vouvray every year, or fifteen million bottles. On average, fifty-five percent were sparkling, and forty-five percent were still. Dry Vouvray had nine grams of residual sugars per liter. Semi-dry had fifteen grams, while sweet and fortified liquors had fifty grams.

"Oh, I forgot to tell you about Les Bournais, with its unique silty clay soil over limestone. This is the land of bubbly wines, very light and delicate. Over time, they develop candied fruit aromas with a touch of sweet floral, which enhances the freshness."

Benjamin glanced at Virgile again. He was fidgeting.

"That's enough, boss. I won't be able to remember much more."

"And that makes me sad," the winemaker said, turning onto the road leading to Château de Tremblay.

When they arrived, Benjamin saw that the police had cordoned off the meadow used as a parking lot the night of the party, as well as the wine cellar. Several TV-station trucks were just outside the meadow, and photographers and reporters were arguing with a broad-shouldered officer of impressive height who had obviously been stationed there to keep them from getting in.

"Sure is a peaceful place," Virgile said. "Isn't that what you called it?"

Benjamin turned off the engine. He could deal with Virgile's teasing during their ride, but now that they were faced with the reality of what had happened here, he wasn't in the mood for any cracks from his assistant.

"It does, indeed, seem that you're running out of memory, son. I said it was a place where one could pause and recharge. Do you think you could do that? Pause, I mean."

10

Benjamin and Virgile showed their identifications and were allowed to head toward the château after the police officer called the owner.

"I'm sure the forensics team is combing the corridor where Simone was found," the winemaker said as they walked up the steps. "I bet they have dozens of people down there. David has one of the most beautiful tufa-tunnel cellars in the region. It's not comparable to the sumptuous subterranean meanderings of the Huet mansion, of course, but it can house several thousand bottles."

Benjamin and Virgile found the actor slumped in a squat armchair upholstered in purple velvet. He was oozing fatigue and anger and wearing the same expression that had contributed largely to the success of a film he had made in his early years.

"Hello, gentlemen," he let out without getting up. He motioned to a distinguished-looking man with white hair who was sitting in a nearby chair. "This is Dr. Molinier, my medicine man."

Benjamin recognized him. He had seen him at the party, talking to a sixtyish woman in a black sheath. The winemaker had noted his reserve, which stood out in the crowd of style-conscious Parisians who worshipped the cult of youth, spiteful gossip, and fashion. And now he remembered who he was: the renowned cardiac surgeon who had become David's close friend after performing an emergency bypass on him.

David had been coping with a demanding shoot by losing his temper at the slightest provocation and smoking nearly three packs of cigarettes a day. He was hypertensive when he arrived at the hospital, and that he hadn't died was something of a miracle. But, in fact, David had recovered—with panache. The two men had become close, and David leaned heavily on his physician, even though he tended to ignore the doctor's cautionary advice about eating and drinking.

"Dr. Molinier has just arrived," David said. "Have a seat. Something to drink?"

"No, thank you," Benjamin said. "We were at François Pinon's place yesterday, and we didn't do much spitting. I'll wait till this afternoon."

David nodded. "I know his stuff. It's one of the best. Maybe someday I'll be able to compete with him. He's one hell of a vintner."

"I have a lot of respect for his work," Benjamin said. "And I wanted Virgile to meet him and taste on site."

"You're so right. That's how we must train the kids. Nothing like tasting straight from the barrel!"

Virgile shifted in his chair, and Benjamin could read his mind. By now, Virgile had tasted from many barrels. It was one thing for Benjamin to call him "son," but he was no kid. Still, the winemaker imagined that his assistant was excited by the opportunity to spend time with the famous actor. He had told Benjamin about the cinema in Bergerac where he had seen quite a few films in both French and English.

David interrupted the winemaker's thoughts. "Frankly, Benjamin, I have neither the desire nor the strength to talk about our project right now."

"Of course, David. It's not why I came. I wanted to check on you. You must be beside yourself with worry. Our wine project can wait."

"Yes, we'll talk later. You'll be here for a while —am I right? We'll find a moment to visit the parcel. In your own way, like Molinier, you're a medicine man. You work miracles!"

"Except I don't need gloves to operate, and, excuse the macabre allusion, my goal is accumulating dead soldiers for my clients."

Molinier laughed. "Ah yes, a full wine cellar pleases the collector, but it's the emptying of the bottle that pleases him most. And growers are always happy to see empty bottles. Unfortunately, that doesn't go for you, David, as the key in your case is moderation."

David scowled at the doctor. "I can handle my drinking. Now excuse me for being rude, but I need to know how Simone's doing."

Benjamin couldn't hide his surprise. "So you haven't gone to the hospital?" he asked.

"No, Benjamin, I haven't. My presence at the hospital would draw too much attention. Can you imagine all the photographers and television crews besieging the staff if they got wind of it? I want the doctors and nurses to concentrate on Simone. Besides, I couldn't bear seeing her hooked up to all those machines."

The actor's expression changed from anger to sorrow, and Benjamin thought he saw tears welling in his eyes. "It's too much, Benjamin. Simone was so vibrant. How could this happen?"

Molinier, still composed despite David's rebuke, cleared his throat. "I went in David's stead." He reached over and put a hand on the actor's arm. "She's critical but holding her own. I talked to the doctor who's in charge of her case. He's a young man, but competent."

"And?"

"And… He couldn't tell me much more, other than her coma isn't irreversible."

The actor sank deeper into his chair and wiped his face, as if to erase the signs of his fatigue. "And that's supposed to reassure me?"

"Not at all. You never know what the outcome will be, and I wouldn't want to give you false hope. But I can tell you that it's probably a temporary state, especially since the paramedics knew exactly what to do, and the medical team responded quickly when Simone arrived at the emergency room. As soon as they got her into intensive care, they gave her glucose, put her on oxygen, ran the blood work, and ordered an electrocardiogram. In short, they did their job."

"Meaning what?" David mumbled.

"It means we just have to wait, especially because the tests they've run so far haven't shown anything we didn't already know."

"What was it that they already knew?"

"Simone definitely consumed a great deal of alcohol. The blood tests confirm this, but…"

"But what?"

"But I don't think she drank enough to induce nearly fatal alcohol poisoning. There had to be something else. I've discussed this at length with a colleague who has his own thoughts."

"Give it to me straight, Molinier. It looks like you're holding back, and you know very well that you can talk frankly with me. I hate people who beat around the bush."

"I know, David. I know. Let's just say there's no convincing evidence that would explain how Simone wound up this way, but it's precisely the lack of tangible evidence that puts us on the right track."

"That's how it is sometimes," Benjamin suggested. "In fact, the absence of proof always speaks volumes, in the sense that the unexplainable encourages us to dig deeper."

"I imagine you encounter the same problems in your oenology, Mr. Cooker."

"It happens more than you'd think."

David cut in. "It takes a hell of a lot of time for you to get to the point, Molinier. What are your conclusions?"

The doctor's jaw clenched almost impercepti-
bly. "As you know, my area of specialization is
cardiology. My colleague, who's not a cardiologist,
offered a supposition I hadn't thought of." Molinier
paused and looked directly at his audience. "So,
gentlemen, have you ever heard of GHB?"

No one said a word.

He answered for them. "GHB is the acronym
for gamma hydroxybutyrate, also called Liquid X
or liquid ecstasy. You may have read stories about
date-rape drugs. Does that ring a bell?"

Still no response. David frowned. Benjamin
folded his arms, and Virgile looked impassive.

"It's derived from GBL, short for gamma-Bu-
tyrolactone. By mixing GBL with a base, usually
caustic soda, you get GHB. The 4-hydroxybutyrate
of sodium was once used as a general anesthetic
and a treatment for insomnia, especially in cases of
narcolepsy. And it has an additional pharmaceuti-
cal application that the French surgeon Henri La-
borit developed in the early nineteen sixties: it was
our first authentic anti-depressant/anti-anxiety
medication. It was largely replaced by benzodi-
azepines and tricyclic anti-depressants, but in recent years it has found new favor in some psychiatric circles."

David. stopped him again. "Too much information, Molinier! Keep it simple. All this scientific crap's making me feel like I'm being taken for an idiot!"

"Nothing could be further from my intention," the doctor answered.

Benjamin couldn't help admiring Molinier for maintaining his bedside manner with this impatient patient.

"I just wanted to give you a bit of history and science before getting to the crux," the doctor continued. "GHB has been used as a general anesthetic and as a treatment for narcolepsy, alcoholism, and depression. But it's also used illegally as a date-rape drug, which I mentioned, and as an athletic-performance enhancer. And it's easy to obtain on the Internet, especially on American websites."

"So, conceivably, anyone could get it?" Benjamin said, leaning forward.

"Absolutely. Illicit traffic is widespread. Bodybuilders take it because it allows them to train harder. Outside the world of bodybuilding, plenty of people seek it for its socializing effect. After a single dose, the user feels uninhibited, liberated. That's why it's called liquid ecstasy. And there's a noted improvement in sexual performance. The aphrodisiac properties haven't been proved, but the user has a sense of euphoria, if you know what I mean."

"We know exactly what you mean," David grumbled. "I smell a rat."

"This isn't a drug you want to fool around with, though," Molinier said. "In low doses there's the risk of nausea, a slowing of heart and respiratory rates, hypertension, serious problems with coordination and balance, hallucinations, and drowsiness. Overdoses can result in loss of consciousness and coma. Remember? I said it's used as a general anesthetic. And that's why it's called a date-rape drug. Many women have been assaulted after unwittingly ingesting the substance with alcohol and passing out. This isn't uncommon, since illicit GHB is found in all the fashionable nightclubs in London, Amsterdam, and, more recently, Paris."

"What are you telling me—that Simone was raped?"

"We don't know. They conducted a rape-kit exam in the emergency room, but the results aren't back yet."

"I swear, if she was raped…" The vein in David's temple was throbbing.

"Calm down, David. We don't have the results yet. We must wait and see. That's all I can tell you for the time being."

Benjamin was still leaning forward in his chair. "You mentioned a lack of convincing evidence. I assume you're talking about the GHB, not the rape kit."

The surgeon looked at the winemaker with an almost relieved expression. "You're a scientist, Mr. Cooker, and you're approaching this logically. You've got your finger on a fundamental problem with GHB: it's not easy to detect."

"So, someone who's been drugged might not know it?"

"Correct. GHB does have a salty, soapy taste. But once GHB's in alcohol, it can't be tasted anymore. To make matters worse, after GHB has been ingested, it's hard to detect. Its half-life, the time needed for a drug's plasma concentration to go down by fifty percent, is an impressive twenty-seven minutes. Less than five percent of the original amount remains in the body after two hours."

Virgile cleared his throat, and the three other men turned to him. "Therefore, it's difficult—if not impossible—to prove that GHB was used as a weapon in a sexual assault. Without bruising or other evidence, it could look like consensual sex. Or a case of he-said, she-said."

Molinier nodded. "Exactly, young man."

"But even if there's no GHB in the blood-stream, you could find traces of it in a glass, couldn't you?"

"I'm sorry, I'm not a specialist in that area," the doctor said.

"Shouldn't the glasses from the party be ana-lyzed? The cops should be notified."

"Too late," David said. "Everything was washed, dried, and put away."

"And the police allowed that?" Benjamin asked, astonished. "They didn't tell you to leave everything as is?"

"The cleanup started before Simone was found. I had drunk too much and gone to bed. I believe my personal assistant told you that she tried to wake me, but I couldn't be roused. The security guard who called the paramedics told them to be discreet. After the ambulance left with Simone, the caterers and house staff finished their work and went home. The police arrived several hours later."

Benjamin shook his head and folded his arms.

"If I may ask one more question, doctor," Vir-gile said. "You say bodybuilders use this substance.

I assume you're talking about the guys who do competitions and serious things like that. Is it used by many ordinary fellows who just go to the gym and want to look good?"

Before he could answer, someone knocked on the door. David rose heavily from his chair. "Yes?"

"Inspector Blanchet, from the Tours Police Department."

David let him in. The middle-aged inspector, wearing a mousey polyester suit and pistachio-colored shirt, gave Benjamin, Virgile, and Molinier a nod before turning to David. "As you know, my men have been collecting evidence in the wine cellar," he said. "There was a wall in the second tunnel that sounded hollow. On the right side, four meters past the entrance to the passageway…"

"Past the shelves of sweet wines?" the actor asked.

"I couldn't tell you if they were sweet. They were bottles lined up on dusty shelves. We went ahead and probed. Then we did a little digging…"

David glared at him. "Forgive me, but you could have asked my permission!"

The inspector remained poker-faced. "I thought about it, but I didn't have the opportunity. My men whacked the wall a few times, and a rock gave way."

"What the hell is going on?"

"First one rock, then another. I'm afraid part of the wall collapsed."

"You police officers feel entitled to do whatever you please!" David shouted. "I won't hold my breath waiting for the Ministry of the Interior to compensate me!"

"That's the ministry's job, not mine." The inspector waited a moment. "Mr. Navarre, we made a rather shocking discovery."

Benjamin exchanged a glance with Virgile.

"Don't tell me you found a buried treasure," the actor said. "That would be the only good piece of news we've had all day!"

"Yes, something buried," the inspector answered. "But it was no treasure."

11

Benjamin, Virgile, David, and Dr. Molinier followed Inspector Blanchet down the stone steps to the sizable cave housing the château's wine cellar. Here, the wines were stored at an ideal year-round temperature.

Caverns such as this one, both natural and manmade, dotted the Loire Valley. In some cases, the limestone had been mined for use in the region's châteaus, churches, and castles.

As he walked along, Benjamin mused on what the enterprising residents of the Loire Valley had done with these hidden spaces. Les Hautes Roches, once a monastery, had been built against a backdrop of soft tuffeau limestone. Today it was a luxury hotel with a Michelin-starred restaurant and guest rooms tucked into the rock. Bourre, near Amboise, was home to a four-hundred-kilometer subterranean mushroom farm that produced varieties including oyster, blue foot, and shiitake. And then there was the Troglodytic Valley of Goupillières, three authentic farms built into the tufa hollows. He had gone there once with Margaux, and she had said it reminded her of a Hobbit village.

A poke in the ribs interrupted the winemaker's thoughts. It was Virgile. "Boss," he whispered, using his chin to point toward the police inspector. Blanchet was examining something on the floor. Benjamin couldn't quite make it out, as it was hidden by the rubble of the felled wall. He stepped closer and saw what the inspector was staring at.

Bones: two femurs, ribs, radius and ulna, sternum, pubis. And a skull, grinning at them.

"What the hell?" David shouted. "This must be some kind of joke."

"It's no joke, I assure you," Blanchet said. "It's a human skeleton. About five feet seven, teeth intact. Broken clavicle. We need to know who this person was and how he or she got here."

"You expect me to know?" Even in the dim lighting, Benjamin could see that David's face was red.

Dr. Molinier put an arm around his shoulder. "Calm down. Getting upset won't solve anything."

David wrenched himself free. "I have no idea who this is, Inspector. Nor do I know how it got here. I suppose you'll be tearing up my cellar even more now."

Blanchet didn't bat an eye. "We need to identify the skeleton and determine how it got here." He held out a piece of jewelry—a chain with a medal. "Can you tell me anything about this? It's the Virgin Mary and child. We assume the deceased was wearing it."

"You tell me, Inspector." David looked around his cellar, assessing the damage. Broken bottles littered the floor. He ran a hand through his cropped hair. "Haven't we been through enough?"

No one answered. Finally, Benjamin spoke. "How long do you expect to be here, Inspector? Mr. Navarre would like to get things back in order as soon as possible."

Blanchet dropped the chain into a plastic evidence bag. "I think we can wrap up our work here by the end of the day. Of course, the skeleton must be transported to the morgue. That will happen either today or tomorrow." He turned to David. "Mr. Navarre, you and your friends can leave now. I'll be in touch with any additional questions."

The four men made their way out of the wine cellar. As soon as they were back in David's study, the actor pulled Benjamin aside. "Benjamin, you've got to help me. I don't trust that guy Blanchet. He'll try to pin this on me."

"I don't see how he can do that, David. The skeleton looked like it's been there for decades. You haven't owned your place that long."

"It doesn't matter, Benjamin. I've got to get to the bottom of this before I'm dragged into any more hassles. Can you imagine what the media will do if they learn about this?"

"You have a point. But what do you want me to do about it?"

"I want you to find out who that skeleton belonged to and how it got here."

"David, identifying bones isn't my area of expertise."

"Benjamin, don't kid me. I'm familiar with the crimes you've solved. I know you've got your hands full with that documentary, but please help me. You can hold off on studying my parcel. And I'll pay you three times your going rate!"

Benjamin sighed. "That won't be necessary. I'll look into it, but I'm not making any promises."

"Thank you, Benjamin. Please, see what you can find out. From you, that's the same as delivering the goods."

12

"I don't know, boss," Virgile said as they made their way back to the car. "How can we handle the skeleton with everything else we've got going? Liza's expecting us to spend the rest of the day with her, and we've just begun filming."

"I'm aware of that, Virgile. But if David is sincere about putting off the work on his parcel, we might be able to deal with the skeleton and keep Liza happy. Maybe we can get David pointed in the right direction, and then he can hire someone else— someone who specializes in well-aged bones instead of well-aged wines—to finish the investigation."

The winemaker's weak attempt at humor didn't even elicit a smile. "I'm sure he'll appreciate whatever we can do, boss."

Virgile looked like he had something on his mind, but Benjamin didn't ask. He was beginning to feel overwhelmed. The demands of the film shoot,

Simone's assault, the skeleton, and what appeared to be David's declining emotional state were all on his mind. Benjamin was missing Grangebelle and its peace and continuity. The winemaker needed a quiet drive to reestablish a sense of order, so he didn't attempt to converse with Virgile during their drive to the spot Liza had designated.

They spent the remainder of the day on location, complying with Liza's requests as she arranged the scenes needed in the editing phase of the project. This entailed filming several shots that would link the sequences: opening the door of the convertible, closing it, repeating the opening and closing a dozen times—from a lower angle or a higher angle--faster, slower, almost as fast, but not too fast, either. "Thank you, gentlemen. Could you please do it again, but while starting the engine this time?" It wasn't really a request, but rather a friendly yet authoritative suggestion.

Benjamin grumbled and sighed, making no attempt to conceal his weariness, while Virgile just went along. Liza apparently felt she could count on Virgile's cooperation. He didn't seem nervous and made none of the little self-conscious gestures common for beginners. But what Liza didn't notice, Benjamin did. He was staring at Fabrice.

At sundown, when they could no longer work, the winemaker suggested that they have dinner at the Grand Vatel in Vouvray. Liza declined, saying she was tired. She would have something in her room.

Annoying as she was with her sundry expectations, Benjamin couldn't help respecting this woman, a consummate professional who would never make the kind of money her less-talented male peers were earning. On her budget, she couldn't treat five people to a meal at the Grand Vatel. A truck stop or snack bar for food and a low-cost hotel on the side of the highway for lodging—that was all the Open Air budget would allow for. And yet Liza carried on with confidence and pride.

They said their good-byes and parted ways.

"I suppose the shoot went as well as it could," Benjamin said as he opened the car door. "You're a natural, Virgile. What was it, though, with those looks you were giving Fabrice? If I didn't know better, I'd think you'd switched teams."

Virgile laughed. "Where on earth did you hear that expression?"

"As I said, you don't give me enough credit. I do read. Now what about Fabrice?"

"Nothing, boss. He just seems to get around a lot."

Benjamin waited for more information, but none came. He let it go, and they spent the rest of the drive back to Château de Pray listening to Debussy's *Prélude à l'après midi d'un faune*. Once there, they freshened up in their rooms and met again on the ground floor, where they came face-to-face with Lee Friedman.

"Ah, once again we meet," Lee said.

"I didn't know you were staying here," Benjamin said, shaking the screenwriter's hand.

"I'm taking a short break from Paris. I was on my way to the salon for a drink. Would you care to join me?"

"Why not?" Benjamin said.

As soon as they settled in their armchairs, a smiling staff member arrived and offered them a Bonnezeaux.

"As long as it's a Château de Fesles," Benjamin said.

"That it is," she said, filling their glasses.

She left, and Lee turned to Benjamin. "I know how you love your cigars. It must be difficult to find a place to light up these days."

The winemaker shook his head. "It seems no one puts up with cigar smoke anymore. A peppery

Cohibas would have gone nicely with this 2007 Château de Fesles."

"I believe the smoke makes some people sick," Lee said.

"To be honest, Lee, I'm of the opinion that some people just think it makes them sick. I quote Friedrich Durrenmatt. 'Without tolerance, our world turns into hell.'"

"Now, Benjamin, don't you think that applies to you, as well?"

The winemaker chuckled. "Touché, my friend. And the lack of a cigar won't keep me from admiring this fine wine." He studied the honeyed color and sniffed the aromas of ripe apricot and exotic fruit on a mineral base. He sipped. The Bonnezeaux was intense and rich. Bernard Germain, who owned the estate from 1996 to 2008, could transform a grape into gold.

As the winemaker began to relax, he noticed that Lee didn't seem quite as attentive. The screenwriter was known for his insights and quick wit, but now he seemed distracted, despondent, even. "So how are you, Lee? If you don't mind my saying, you seem a little off your game."

Lee sighed. "You don't miss a beat, do you, Benjamin. To answer your question, I've been better."

"What's going on?"

"How long do you have?"

Benjamin smiled. "As long as you need. Let's order another glass of the Château de Fesles." And so the winemaker listened patiently while Lee related his troubles: a year spent dealing with a sordid divorce, betrayals, deception, and slander meted out by a wicked and manipulative spouse, in-laws blinded by hate, and friends who claimed to be impartial but proved to be incredibly stupid. He had lost his home and custody of his son. A criminal complaint filed by his wife hadn't gone to trial yet, and paying for the lawyer alone was becoming cost-prohibitive. His work was his only distraction, and too much wine at night was his only comfort.

Benjamin felt for his writer friend, a man in his fifties undone by the woman he had trusted most in this world. He had been betrayed by someone else, as well. According to Benjamin's publisher, David Navarre had helped himself to a quickie with Lee's wife at a dinner party in Paris. And then she had the impudence to tell Lee.

Benjamin winced at the recollection. Still, Lee and David didn't seem uncomfortable with each other. He would have thought Lee would be furious, and David would be doing his best to avoid the man he had stabbed in the back. But then again, Lee tended to keep things bottled up. Maybe he was too humiliated and didn't want to admit what had happened. And perhaps David was feeling guilty and making up for his indiscretion by trying to get Gayraud moving on the screenplay.

Benjamin silently gave thanks for his own blessings: Elisabeth, his home, his smart and talented daughter, the rewards of his work, and, yes, even Virgile. He banished the memory and lightened the mood. "We were planning to dine at the Grand Vatel," he said. "Would you like to come along?"

"Indeed, why go our separate ways?" Lee said. "But I had lunch there with Gayraud."

"Oh? Did you make any headway on your contract?"

Lee shook his head. "I'm afraid not. He holds out the carrot, but it's always out of reach. And, of course, I picked up the check."

"So sorry, Lee," Benjamin said. "Tonight, dinner's on me." He turned to Virgile. "Any preferences?"

"It doesn't matter boss. But the sooner we eat, the better. I'm starving."

They decided to stay at Château de Pray and went out to the terrace, even though it was a bit chilly.

"Getting back to your project, Lee—I'm intrigued," Benjamin said after they placed their orders. "Why a *Vineyard Plot* screenplay?"

Lee chuckled. "I'd think you'd be flattered, Benjamin. The character's based on you. And the book's a bestseller, remember? It's a no-brainer—following the book with a film."

"I'm more surprised than flattered. I like to think of myself as the staid sort."

"You may dress conservatively, Benjamin, but staid isn't you."

This was more talk about himself than he cared to indulge. The winemaker changed the subject just as their dinners were arriving. "So, are you planning a lengthy stay here?"

"I haven't decided," Lee said, picking at his veal shank with Loire Valley spinach and goat cheese. "I wanted to attend David's party, as he'd told me Gayraud would be there. Beyond these next few days, however, I don't know. It's ironic, isn't it, that I came for a respite, and everything here has blown up. Who would have guessed there'd be a tragedy at David's château?" Lee shook his head. "There's no peace in the valley."

"No, there isn't," Benjamin said before taking a bite of his artichokes and whelk.

Virgile tilted his head. "'Peace in the Valley.' Isn't that an American song?"

"Yes, it is," Lee said. "Written in 1937 for Mahalia Jackson. 'There will be peace in the valley for me some day. There will be peace in the valley for me, oh, Lord, I pray. There will be no sadness, no sorrow, no trouble, I see.'"

Benjamin put his fork down. "I never would have pegged you as a fan of gospel music."

Lee smiled. "There's a lot you don't know about me, Benjamin, my taste in music included. I've been a French citizen for quite a while now, but my roots are American. Elvis Presley recorded 'Peace in the Valley' in 1957. He sang it on the *Ed Sullivan Show* and asked his fans to send emergency aid for the more than two hundred thousand refugees who fled Hungary after the Soviet invasion. Many of those refugees settled in London."

Benjamin nodded. "London has a very large Hungarian population. As a matter of fact, the last time Elisabeth and I visited my father, he took us to a wonderful restaurant in Soho. I had cabbage stuffed with minced pork, sauerkraut, and bacon. For dessert, Elisabeth and I shared *dobos torta.*"

"What's that, boss?"

"Cake topped with caramel."

"Mmm, sounds delicious," Virgile said. "Let's make sure we check the dessert menu."

Lee wiped his mouth. "At any rate, I find solace in that song, especially now."

"'No sadness, no sorrow.' Isn't that what we all seek?" Benjamin said. "But there's no avoiding it. People fail us, abandon us, deceive us. Life takes unexpected turns…"

Virgile sighed, and Benjamin looked over at him. "What is it, son?"

"Ah, boss, do you think we could change the subject? Maybe there's no avoiding sadness and sorrow. But could we could give it a rest while we're enjoying our meal and looking forward to dessert?"

Benjamin smiled. Virgile knew how to get a conversation back on track. "All right, Virgile. No more talk of sadness and sorrow." But the winemaker didn't have a chance.

"Have you heard anything about Simone?" Lee asked abruptly. "Do they know how she wound up unconscious in the cellar?"

Benjamin played coy. "I really don't have any solid information. But there's speculation that she was drugged."

Lee put his fork down. His hand was trembling. "Drugged? With what?"

"The police haven't released anything yet. Let me ask, Lee: do you know anyone who would want to do that to her?"

"How would I know? You'd be better off asking that asshole director Max Armond, who'd been pushing her to the brink, or her boyfriend David. They could get their hands on any drug they wanted."

"I'm sure the police will be questioning them." Benjamin took his last bite. "At any rate, let's follow Virgile's advice and order dessert. I hear the hot soufflé and blackcurrant sorbet are excellent."

The three men made their selections, and Benjamin suggested that they end the evening with a very old Château-de-Prada Armagnac made by his friend Philippe de Bouglon.

The winemaker was about to note the golden color and candied apricot and mandarin aroma when he heard giggling at a nearby table. He glanced over. Two women, one with curly auburn hair and the other with a long dark-brown ponytail, were grinning and staring at Virgile. Next to the one with the ponytail was a magazine opened to a photograph.

"Virgile, they're pointing at you," Benjamin said.

"Seriously?" Virgile turned their way and then looked back at Benjamin. His face was flushed. "That magazine, boss—there's a photograph of me dancing with Simone Margerolle."

Before Benjamin could stop him, Virgile got up and walked over to the women's table. He said something and returned with the magazine.

"Let's have a look," Benjamin said, grabbing the publication. Sure enough, it was his assistant—embracing the actress, whose cheek was resting on his shoulder. The sensuous mouth, half-closed eyes, loose hair, and pearls of sweat—she had never looked more seductive. And the caption? "Last dance."

Benjamin couldn't hide his shock. "What rag is this?" he said, turning to the cover. It was *Voici!*. He looked at the photo once again and saw that it was part of an entire article on the eventful night at David Navarre's château. "I can't imagine how they got this in so quickly. They must have stopped a press run. At least they didn't name you, Virgile."

"There was a magazine photographer at the party, boss. But I didn't see him taking pictures of me."

"Apparently because you were very busy canoodling with the actress." Benjamin could feel his blood pressure rising. "Do you know what publicity like this could do to us? Cooker & Co. has a reputation to maintain! You said you spoke briefly and shared a dance. That was it."

"Honest, boss, that's all that happened."

Lee picked up the magazine and looked through it quickly. "What's your surname, Virgile? Lanssien, isn't it?"

"Yes, with two s's," Virgile said.

"With such a name, you'd be expected to have more wisdom. But then again, I've been caught with my pants down one or two times."

"But it wasn't like that—not at all like that," Virgile protested. "Boss, you've got to believe me."

Lee looked at Benjamin. "A photograph taken out of context can not only do a lot of harm, but also cast suspicion on the wrong person."

Turning to Virgile, Lee asked, "I suppose you've read some Cato the Elder?"

"Never heard of him."

"You're very well read, Benjamin. You must know what I'm referring to."

Benjamin sipped his Armagnac to soothe his nerves. Then he understood. "'If you catch your wife in adultery, you can kill her with impunity.'"

"Exactly."

13

She was calm and reassuring. For more than half an hour, Benjamin listened to Elisabeth. He had begun their phone conversation with pleasantries. He didn't want to worry her, after all. But a few minutes later he was pouring out his troubles. At crucial times such as this, Elisabeth was the one he needed most.

Benjamin reviewed the situation. The newspapers and television and radio stations had followed up on the article in *Voici!* and were expanding on it. Where they were getting their information, he had no idea. The lion's share was wrong.

At dawn Inspector Blanchet had arrived at Château de Pray to arrest Virgile. They had handcuffed him and taken him away in an unmarked car. Two detectives stayed behind to search the room.

"How did they know Virgile was at Château de Pray?" Elisabeth asked.

"Blanchet saw us yesterday at David's place. It wasn't hard for him to make the connection."

"From what you've told me, all the police have is a photo of Virgile dancing with the woman. Dancing's hardly a crime, much less evidence in an attempted homicide investigation, if that's the charge they're considering. There must be more believable suspects. I'm sure this mistake will be corrected quickly. They have no reason to hold Virgile."

Benjamin knew Elisabeth was fond of his assistant. She had to be fretting too, but he couldn't detect any worry in her tone. How he loved her!

"And what about David?" she asked.

Lee's innuendo flashed in Benjamin's head. Had David seen Simone dancing seductively with Virgile, perhaps with other men, as well? Had he assumed the wrong thing? Was he that insecure, that jealous?

"What do you mean, Elisabeth?"

"I imagine he's livid."

"I can't get hold of him. He's not answering my calls. I need to see him to explain that this is an unfortunate misunderstanding. Virgile would never..."

"It must be very embarrassing to see your wife —I mean your mistress or lover... What is she to him, anyway?"

"We'll call her his companion," Benjamin said.

"Oh, yes, that's better, more elegant. At any rate, put yourself in his place. It must be embarrassing to see a photo of your companion in a suggestive embrace with a handsome young man, especially your winemaker's assistant. And the photo was taken in his own home!"

"That idiot Virgile—he should have known better than to sully our reputation." Benjamin was getting angry again. "And tell me this, Elisabeth: why would he allow himself to be seduced that way when he was supposedly pining for our daughter?"

Benjamin didn't hear anything. Finally, Elisabeth spoke. "Virgile and I talked on the phone last week. He calls from time to time."

"Really, Elisabeth? Why haven't you told me about these phone calls?"

"Benjamin, I don't find it necessary to tell you about every little thing in my life, and, frankly, I don't like your tone."

Benjamin took a sip of water to calm himself. "Forgive me, Elisabeth. You're right. So, what did my assistant tell you?"

"Margaux posted a photo of herself on Instagram. She was with a man, and, according to

Virgile, they seemed quite taken with each other. He was upset."

Benjamin sipped again. "A man? Who was this guy?"

"I have no idea, Benjamin. I don't even know if they're in a relationship. But after seeing the photo in *Voici!* I'm sure you understand that a picture can be deceiving. I plan to wait. If Margaux thinks I should know about him, she'll tell me."

"And when you find out, would you show me the courtesy of sharing the information? Why am I always the last to know about these things? Meanwhile, my very livelihood's at stake!"

"Sweetheart, there's no need to be overly dramatic. Cooker & Co. will weather this storm, just as it has weathered every other storm. And admit it. You're more concerned about Virgile than your firm's reputation. Virgile probably did nothing to attract the actress. She happened to find him at a very vulnerable moment. Besides, you know girls find him irresistible."

"Please, Elisabeth, stop excusing him. This time it's really beyond the pale. Carrying on openly with a woman who's a disaster waiting to happen! He may be irresistible, but mostly he can't resist. As far as I'm concerned, it has nothing to do with Margaux. He's an idiot, a big idiot!"

"I'll say it again: a photo can easily be taken out of context. And this could have been a trap."

"I agree, especially since he never denied talking and dancing with little Miss Margerolle."

"So, you see, he's been transparent with you. He told you about it himself, without your even having to inquire."

"True enough. Besides, how can anyone get angry with him?" Benjamin cracked. "He's so attractive!"

"Stop, Benjamin. If I didn't know you better, I'd think you were envious. I'm not the only one who says that about Virgile. Many of my friends have told me they think he's handsome and charming."

"Your friends are adept at lending this lothario qualities he doesn't deserve. Meanwhile, he's behind bars. And, oh, there's something else: the police happened to discover a skeleton in Navarre's cellar, and he wants me to find out how it got there—as though I didn't have enough to deal with already."

Elisabeth sighed. "You have your hands full, Benjamin, but I know you'll take care of everything. Virgile will be out in no time. The right person will be arrested, and you'll finish your work. I'll be waiting for you at Grangebelle with *blanquette de veau* and, if you're lucky, *cannelés*.

"*Cannelés?*" Benjamin's mouth was already watering, and the prospect brightened his mood. He and Elisabeth ended their conversation with sweet parting words and a promise to call each other as soon as possible.

14

Benjamin threw on his jacket and hurried down the staircase, almost tipping over the suit of armor in front of the stained-glass window. The Open Air team was waiting in the courtyard, near their van.

"So, you know," Benjamin said when he saw their faces.

"Yes, we've seen the newspapers," Liza answered. "But it won't keep us from filming. We'll take care of Virgile's absence when we edit. No one will notice."

Benjamin nodded. "After all, it's the wine that matters. We're just oral historians, conveyors of influence. The true star of your documentary is the wine."

"But I must admit that Virgile's presence brings a lot to our project. Besides, he's quite photogenic."

Benjamin's mood turned dark again. "Shit, not you too!" he thundered, not caring how rude he sounded.

He spun on his heel and marched over to his Mercedes. The gravel flew as he sped down the drive. Once on the highway, he let up on the gas pedal, but he continued to curse female gullibility and his assistant's pheromones.

The filming was scheduled to take place at the estate of la Fontainerie, where Catherine Dhoye Deruet was awaiting them. Catherine was one of the first women to take charge of a family estate in the Vouvray appellation. Benjamin wanted to underscore the strides made by female winemakers in the Loire Valley. According to some estimates, women accounted for upwards of forty percent of the region's vintners.

Aware that Catherine might be uncomfortable around the film crew, Benjamin made it clear that he was there as a colleague and friend, not as a member of the production team. Eventually, everyone relaxed and became oblivious to the director and her assistants.

Liza seemed pleased at Benjamin's ability to make an interviewee shine without becoming invisible himself. With a nod of her head, she told Fabrice to move in for a closeup. The cameraman complied.

While Catherine offered tastings of a 2008 moelleux from the cuvée Coteaux les Brûlés, the winemaker outlined her career path, which resembled that of François Pinon. After pursuing an education as an agricultural engineer, she worked at a food-process engineering school near Paris. When her parents decided to retire and rent their vineyards to neighbors, she didn't hesitate to return to the estate, which had been in the family since the seventeen hundreds, and take over operations.

"But your parents weren't living on the property, were they," said Benjamin, who knew the family well but let Catherine tell her own story.

"No, they weren't on the property. The house adjoining the cellar hadn't had any occupants for fifty years or so."

"What changes did you initiate when you took over?"

"No major changes in the cellar, except for updating the grape press. It still worked well, but it was very old. We modernized gradually. There was nothing revolutionary about it."

While conversing, Benjamin tasted the moelleux. It had delicate spices on the nose, soon confirmed in the mouth, where they developed into aromas of roasted pineapple. The finish was long, smooth, and round, persistent and fresh.

"Perhaps there was no revolution, but I note a superb evolution in this wine."

Liza gave him an amused wink. The transition was perfect.

"At first, the neighbors watched me with some skepticism," the Dhoye heiress continued. "But little by little, I think I've created a following by developing and improving the cultivation of vines in environmentally sustainable ways. We avoid spraying pesticide whenever we can, and we harvest by hand. My father was already working that way. The main thing is to have a healthy grape and steer clear of chaptalization. From there, everything happens naturally."

"Cut!" shouted Liza, clearly delighted. "You were perfect!"

"That's all you need?" Benjamin asked, a bit frustrated about ending a conversation he wanted to pursue.

"Perfect, I tell you!"

The technicians were already preparing to cross the courtyard and climb the heights of the Fontainerie estate, where they would take additional footage of Benjamin walking the rows of vines.

"If that's all you need, I'll say good-bye," Catherine said. "Please feel free to finish your filming. Enzo, one of my assistants, can help you with anything you need." She turned and walked away.

Still disgruntled, Benjamin looked up and saw that Fabrice and Hugo had arrived at the designated spot. He faithfully followed Liza's instructions to: examine a leaf, scoop up a handful of soil, climb the slope without hunching forward, walk slowly down the hill, avoid squinting when facing the sun, and "fix that shirt collar." He didn't utter a complaint.

But when Liza told him to readjust his collar yet again, Benjamin had had enough. He yanked the clip-on microphone from his jacket. "Okay, that's it!"

"What happened?" Liza asked. "You're not going to leave us like that, are you?"

"Yes, I'm leaving like that! Sorry, Ms. Stechel-mann, I've got better things to do.

15

A stranger would have surmised that peace had been restored at Château de Tremblay. Farm workers paced the northward-running plots. In the distance, a tractor wobbled between rows of chenin vines. Above them, a buzzard circled lazily. The police were gone. By this time, most of the samples collected at the scene had been analyzed in a laboratory smelling of formaldehyde.

Benjamin entered the house without calling out. He didn't encounter anyone and took the flight of steps leading to David Navarre's private rooms. He knocked on the cherry-wood door and turned the knob.

"What the hell are you doing here? Did I invite you?"

The winemaker had expected this. "Hello, David. I came over to find out how Simone's doing."

"She's the same—stable. Do you think you can barge into my home whenever you like?"

"You know very well it's not my habit, but you haven't been answering my calls. I took the liberty to…"

"To come bother me! I don't need anyone making things worse."

"Listen, David. I can only imagine how angry that *Voici!* article must have made you."

"That ass-wipe magazine already has my lawyers on their back! As for your assistant…"

"Let me tell you, my assistant is as furious as you. He's in custody in Tours."

"But just who is that little shit?"

"A very good young man in whom I have total confidence. You'll see for yourself when he comes to help you revive your land and develop your vintage. I believe everything he's told me. He did, indeed, dance with Simone, and they exchanged a few words, but it was nothing more than that."

"The picture tells a different story. Don't waste your breath, Benjamin."

"I know Virgile, and I can assure you that he's an honorable young man from Bergerac who has worked for me for years. Virgile would never drug a girl, and he did nothing untoward the night of your party. He danced with her, that's it."

"I don't know your assistant from Adam, but I have no illusions about Simone's fidelity. I'm familiar with all of her compulsions—more than she realizes."

Benjamin decided to throw caution to the wind. He had to bring it up. "David, I must ask you," he said, looking the actor in the eye. "Who, other than your personal assistant, can verify that you went to bed early that night and slept through everything?"

"What are you suggesting, Benjamin? That I would do that to Simone?" David's face was flushed. "You've got to be kidding. But if you really want to verify—and what an insult that word is— you'll have to ask my assistant if anyone else checked on me. I couldn't tell you. I was out of it."

"I'm sorry, David. I spoke with your assistant while we were waiting for the ambulance, and I have no reason to doubt her. I hope her word is good enough for the authorities." Benjamin waited a moment. "As for Virgile, I vouch for him unconditionally. He's a remarkable professional, and I'd trust him with the keys to my office, without question. In fact, I have. He's incredibly honest and has values I find perfectly acceptable."

Benjamin had said all this firmly, looking straight at David, whose blue eyes were tinged with fine red veins, signs of his pain and loneliness. The actor looked down and said nothing. Then, sighing, he got up and staggered over to a liquor cabinet on the other side of the room.

"What are you drinking, Benjamin?"

"I'm not drinking anything, thank you."

David reached for a bottle of pure malt whiskey. He poured himself a full glass and gulped it down. "I've been getting hammered for more than forty-eight hours now," he said, wiping his mouth. "That's the only way I can cope."

"You shouldn't be doing this to yourself, David. You must keep it together. Simone will need you when she comes out of her coma. And you're not alone. You know you can count on my support."

"When she comes out of her coma? Who knows when that will be? That's if she survives." The actor was about to pour another drink when someone knocked on the door.

"That must be Gayraud. An hour late, as usual."

The producer came in, wearing an unctuous smile. He threw his raincoat over a chair and gave the winemaker a weak handshake. "What a surprise to see you here, Benjamin."

"You're late!" David bellowed before Benjamin could answer. He downed his whiskey.

"Forgive me. I had a meeting with Max Armond and my investors, and I couldn't break free. Then there was heavy traffic on the highway."

"Problems with your fellow schemers and connivers?"

Gayraud ignored the swipe. "They don't want to move ahead until they know what's going on with Simone. As a matter of fact, they're talking about replacing her."

"You're kidding, I hope."

"I managed to pacify them, but we might have to acquiesce. I've got a binder with the photos and bios of possible replacements in case Simone can't finish the job."

"Nobody gives a damn about anyone in this business. I don't care how big you are or how much money you make for them at the box office."

"Listen, it seems wise not to argue. I agree with you: Simone's ideal for the part, and if all goes well, she'll get through this and finish the film. But we must cover our asses and have a replacement lined up. Here's the binder. If you could give me your opinion right away, I'd be appreciative."

Jean-Paul Gayraud placed the large black binder on the coffee table and opened it.

"I'd like your opinion, Benjamin," David said as the producer began flipping through the pages.

"Oh, you're taking your chances with me," the winemaker responded. "I'm very particular."

"How do you like your women?" Gayraud asked.

Benjamin ignored the misogynistic tone. "I like a hint of mystery."

"Well then, you're in luck," said David. "None of these skirts are what they seem. You can count on that. Look at these glamor shots, taken at the best angles and touched up—all of them. And just when you think you've found one who isn't fake, she shows up at the audition and can't act."

They went through the binder methodically, quickly eliminating the actresses who didn't fit the bill. From time to time Benjamin gave his terse opinion. Having known David and a few others in the business, he sensed what they were looking for.

True to form, David didn't beat around the bush. "Too slutty," he'd say, turning the page, or "this one doesn't seem too bright." The next one was awkward-looking, and the one after that had "too much boob." Then there were the actresses who looked anorexic and the ones with bad teeth.

They culled the prospects to five possible re-placements with sufficient theatre experience and successful supporting roles in the previous two years.

"What about this one?" Gayraud said, pointing to a blonde in a tight off-the-shoulder sweater. "Her features are similar to Simone's, although she has a mole near her lip."

"Yes, I see the resemblance," Benjamin said. "Still, she's unique. There's something about her. She has class and an honest face. And yet she looks very... How can I say it?"

"Mysterious?" Gayraud asked.

"Yes, that's the word. If it were up to me, I'd go with this one."

"I agree," David said. "This girl's alluring. And the mole's cute. It sets her apart from the rest."

"I had a hunch you'd pick her," Gayraud said, closing the binder. And I confess, she's my choice, as well. So we'll need to go to Paris. You should watch her audition in person. My fellow connivers, as you call them, want your approval because you'll be working with her closely."

"No can do. I have too much going on here. Besides, Simone's still with us. I refuse to leave as long as she's fighting for her life. Let's wait and see. There's no rush."

"We shouldn't wait too long," Gayraud said.

"Gayraud, you don't seem to remember that I've got the skeleton on my hands too. The cops don't want me taking off." David looked at Benjamin. "And while I'm thinking about it, are you on board with investigating that little matter? A few minutes ago you said I could count on you."

"You got me, David," Benjamin said, shaking his head. "I did say that, didn't I. So, yes, I'll dig up what I can."

"Terrible word play, Benjamin, but thanks."

"Have the police given you any more information I can use to get started?"

"Just this: they said the name Octave was engraved on the back of the medal." David turned to Gayraud. "Once we get to the bottom of the skeleton affair, you should pitch it to our pal Lee Friedman. It would make a great plot for a TV show."

The producer smiled sheepishly.

David looked at Gayraud with incredulity. "You haven't locked up that movie deal yet? You scoundrel! You're going to sign that damned contract and see that he gets paid for his screenplay! Do you want me to buy you the pen?"

"Now just a minute!" the producer shot back. "The financial arrangements are complicated. Very complicated."

David sneered at Gayraud. "You can't let go of a ten-cent coin, can you? You're really a bastard. And what would you do without your whores? The authors, the actors, the technicians? They all hustle while you sit around counting your euros. On top of that, you treat them like shit."

"Give it a rest, David," Gayraud said. "Stop with the melodrama."

For the second time that day, Benjamin had had enough. "Gentlemen, I must leave you now," he said, getting up.

As he walked back to his old Mercedes 280 SL parked across the field, the winemaker perceived an indistinct movement in the thick hedge to his right. He heard two clicks, like sounds from an empty shotgun. Probably a small animal snapping twigs in the woods, he thought. He stopped and stared at the hedge. It rustled.

16

"Those bastards didn't even offer me a sandwich! Just a glass of cloudy water every now and then. I've had nothing to eat since yesterday morning, and I feel like I haven't bathed in a month."

"All the more reason to ride in a convertible," Benjamin said, giving Virgile an affectionate cuff on the chin. "I put the top down so you wouldn't stink up the car."

"Very funny, boss."

Early that morning, Inspector Blanchet had called to tell Benjamin they were letting Virgile go. He had been in custody for more than twenty-four hours, and the police had no reason to hold him any longer. Several interrogations had convinced them that Virgile was neither a killer, nor a rapist—not even a drug user, for that matter. Furthermore, they had no evidence. All they had was the photo of him dancing with Simone. So they released Virgile without so much as an apology, although they hadn't been especially nasty, either.

Now the police had to go back to square one, re-examine the guest list provided by David, check the background of each one, wait for the remaining lab results, reconstruct the sequence of events the evening of the party, look into Simone's past, and establish any and all friendly and professional connections linking the lot of them. The case seemed tortuous, and doubts were growing by the hour. The overly zealous press had cast suspicion on Virgile and given the police the notion they could wrap up the investigation without disentangling a skein whose fibers had probably originated in the affluent quarters of Paris.

During their phone conversation, Inspector Blanchet had said the matter was probably more within the purview of the vice squad, but he preferred to keep it out of their hands. Benjamin intuited that the inspector's reputation and honor were on the line. Blanchet wasn't about to let anyone take over. For the time being, no high-ranking official had summoned him, and no influential people were asking him to avoid smearing certain names or to proceed with caution. So far, so good. Perhaps the matter was simpler than they thought, as no big shots were trying to protect themselves.

"I could eat a gigantic breakfast," Virgile said, tuning the radio to a station he liked. "Coffee, croissants, buttered toast with tons of jam, fried eggs, bacon, a liter of orange juice, and why not a bowl of cereal with fromage blanc?"

"A sort of English breakfast, in fact," suggested Benjamin.

"Absolutely! And how about a slice of roast beef, too?"

"Aside from that, don't you have anything to tell me?"

"What do you want me to tell you?"

"Everything! I want to hear all about it."

"Well, they grilled me, sometimes several at a time, sometimes one at a time. But I was onto their game. It was like being in a second-rate movie. I only told them what you already know. I played the nice guy, a bit of a superficial flirt, even better, a very superficial common flirt!"

"Do you know what one of my favorite countrymen said?"

"Which one? You quote so many. But I'll take a stab: the distant relative convicted of gross indecency or the white supremacist?"

"Please, Virgile, speak more kindly of Oscar Wilde and Winston Churchill."

"Sorry, boss, but it's always seemed kind of surprising to me."

"What's that?"

"That Winston Churchill, who despised the Nazis and was a great defender of freedom and democracy, believed that only whites were entitled to it."

Benjamin didn't say anything. No doubt his assistant thought he had stuck his foot in his mouth. He let Virgile squirm.

"Uh, what I meant to say, boss, was that Oscar Wilde and Winston Churchill were what you'd call flamboyant and controversial. Compared with them, you've led—how can I put it—a quiet life."

Benjamin bit his lip to keep from laughing. "Quiet? That's the image I prefer, but consider this: I've just picked you up from jail, where you were held on suspicion of murder. Over the years we've tripped over one corpse after another, just going about the business of helping wine growers do their job. And we've solved more than a few homicides ourselves."

"Okay, okay, boss," Virgile said, shielding himself as though he were about to get punched. "I'm sorry. What did this famous person say?"

"Oscar Wilde always touched on universal truths: 'The first duty in life is to be as artificial as possible. What the second duty is, no one has yet discovered.'"

"That saying is so typically British. But I don't need to read Oscar Wilde to figure that out for myself."

"Yes, it's very English."

"In a very few words, you Brits manage to express what the French take ten sentences to say. We can't help dragging it out."

"Need I remind you, Virgile, that I'm only half British? My mother was French. But I'll humor you. Give me some examples."

"Well, when a Brit insults someone, he goes straight for the kill without any flourishes. While you'd say 'bloody idiot,' we might say, '*Enculé de bâtard de fils de pute.*' 'You're a sodomite, a bastard, and the son of a prostitute.'"

"You've got me there," said Benjamin. "So tell me: why do you go around saying 'my God' all day? Since you're one hundred percent French, shouldn't it be something wordier?"

"Maybe you're rubbing off on me."

"I can see that abstinence and fasting have made you more pensive, son."

"Well, there are French expressions I like a lot. For example, '*raclure de bidet.*' I don't know how you could translate that into English with the same impact. Toilet scum doesn't quite cut it."

"No, it doesn't."

"The expression's a little vulgar for you, I imagine, but it's effective. What's more, it makes me feel better when I say it."

"I just hope that's never in a crowded café."

"I do have some common sense, boss."

Benjamin was savoring the moment. Virgile was a free man, and the wind whipping against his cheeks felt good. Up ahead, the Château d'Amboise proudly reached toward the sky. For now, all was well.

A few minutes later, Virgile broke his contemplation. "Any news about Simone?"

"I understand her condition hasn't changed," Benjamin answered. "She's in a coma. She's still page-one news, and I imagine she will be for some time."

"I'm really sorry, boss. I hate thinking that anything I did caused bad publicity for Cooker & Co."

"Honestly, it's not my biggest concern. Of course, I was mad at you in the beginning, but Elisabeth calmed me down. She believes in you, Virgile."

"Please thank her for me."

"You can thank her yourself. She'll be appreciative. Women will save you, and they'll ruin you too, son. That seems to be your destiny. It'll present challenges, of course. But to be perfectly honest, I wouldn't mind having that kind of problem now and then."

As they approached Château de Pray, Benjamin spotted a dark bank of clouds in the distance. The threat was veering toward the northeast, once again sparing the sloping Touraine hillsides. He turned right and ascended the road leading to the hotel. The gearbox screeched as he downshifted.

"You seem lost in thought, boss. Anything wrong?"

"No, I was just thinking about something Sacha Guitry said.

"What was that?"

"There are two kinds of women: the ones who are young and pretty, and the ones who still find me handsome."

"Boss, that might apply to your father, but you can't be thinking of yourself. I see the stares you get from good-looking women of all ages. Maybe you don't, but I do."

"Thank you for allowing me a bit of vanity," Benjamin said, parking the car. "Besides, I have Elisabeth. If she finds me handsome, what more could I want?"

"I couldn't agree with you more."

Benjamin started to get out but looked over and saw that Virgile was still sitting in the passenger seat, reluctant to leave.

"Boss, there's something I should have told you earlier," Virgile said.

"Oh?"

"Remember when I asked if I could borrow the car? I needed to run an errand."

"Yes, you were buying hair gel."

"No, I wasn't. I went to the hospital. I wanted to see Simone. There's just something about her. I feel so sorry for her."

"I really didn't believe your story, Virgile, but I figured whatever you were using the car for, it was okay. So, did you see her?"

"Yes, but while I was there, a nurse came in and told me someone else had shown up: a tall, muscular guy with a man bun—you know, a clump of hair on top of his head. I think I caught a glimpse of him in the hallway too. It was Fabrice. It had to be."

"Why would he be there?"

"I've been wondering the same thing. He's a well-built guy. Looks like he works out. It's possible he uses GHB."

Neither of them said anything. Finally, Benjamin spoke. "Perhaps he danced with her…"

Virgile finished for him. "And he dropped something in her Champagne with the intention of hooking up. Maybe he felt guilty after she was found in the cellar and thought he had to see her at the hospital, or maybe he wanted to gauge for himself just how long she'd last."

Benjamin shivered. He and Virgile had been working so closely with the film crew. "The rape-kit results are still out," he said. "We'll have to wait."

Virgile nodded.

They both got out of the car. The morning air smelled earthy and scented with flowers that had just come into bloom. Benjamin breathed it in.

"Boss, there's something else I was wondering. How do you manage to remember all those quotations? Sometimes I get the feeling you make them up."

"I remember them because they appeal to me. But who's to say I always attribute them to the right author?"

"Ah, I hadn't thought of that. However, you're the kind of person who checks his sources."

"At least twice. But Virgile, remember this: don't trust anyone who seems too sure of himself."

17

At Château de Pray, the winemaker watched his assistant wolf down a Rabelaisian breakfast. Then he sat in the garden, making notes while Virgile took a hot shower and shaved.

Virgile joined the winemaker thirty minutes later, wearing a plum-colored sweater with cropped trousers and black tassel loafers.

"We simply can't leave Touraine without visiting Domaine Huet," Benjamin said, tucking his notebook into the breast pocket of his tweed jacket. "I'd planned to do that today, but something's come up. David's insistent that I investigate the skeleton matter, and I can't let him down. He's in a bad way."

"Doesn't Liza have plans for us?"

"I'll call and tell her we're tied up. She'll have to find something else to do."

"Okay, boss. So where do we start?"

Benjamin rose to his feet. "With the medal. David said it's engraved with the name Octave. Let's check the birth and death registries in Vouvray and Montlouis."

"Why Montlouis?"

"David told me his estate belonged to a family that owned properties in both communes at the beginning of the twentieth century, when the Vouvray and Montlouis agricultural zones were still unified."

"Checking the records in both places could take a lot of time, boss. How much do we have?"

"I don't know how much we'll need, but I'm hoping the records are computerized. And there are two of us, so with any luck, it might go more quickly than we think."

They decided to go to Vouvray's town hall first. Once there, Virgile flirted with the clerk, a twentyish woman named Yvette with curly strawberry-blond hair, and she agreed to help. Two hours later, they had come up with scores of deceased Octaves, but each had a grave.

Virgile thanked Yvette and gave her a wink before leaving.

"I see you're still charming the girls, Virgile."

"No, boss. I was just being friendly. And weren't you happy to have her help?"

Although Benjamin didn't approve of the tactics, he was, in fact, grateful. But he didn't comment, and the two men were quiet during the ten-minute drive to Montlouis.

They weren't as lucky there. A retirement-age clerk greeted them. He showed them to the records and walked away. Alone this time, Benjamin and Virgile waded through the birth and death documents. Again, they found many Octaves.

"Bingo!"

Benjamin looked up.

Virgile was nearly jumping out of his chair. "An Octave with no grave, boss!"

The winemaker got up and hurried over to his assistant.

"His name is Octave Pastier. What now?"

"Let's find the town newspaper," Benjamin said, already heading toward the exit. They might have something in their morgue."

As soon as Benjamin gave his name to the newspaper's receptionist, the editor was downstairs, shaking the winemaker's hand. "What a surprise! Benjamin Cooker of the *Cooker Guide*! What brings you here?"

"We're doing a little research, and we have a favor to ask," Benjamin said. "We'd like to use your morgue."

The editor grinned. "We call it the library these days. And certainly you may use it. But may I request a favor in return? Would you agree to a short interview with our food and wine writer before you leave?"

"Fair exchange," Benjamin said. The winemaker and his assistant followed the editor to the library, where they were introduced to the woman in charge.

"This is Alice" the editor said. "She'll help you with whatever you need."

Benjamin thanked him, and Alice showed them how to access the archives.

After an hour of searching, Benjamin found an article from July 1937, which reported the disappearance of Octave Pastier, who had gone fishing near Rochecorbon, at the foot of La-Ville-aux-Dames. Five days later, there was an obituary: six lines on page four.

"Octave Pastier was front-page news on Monday and just six lines on an inside page by Wednesday—a poor slob swimming with the fish," Virgile said.

"Not quite," Benjamin said. "His body wasn't found in the river. It wasn't found anywhere. But they still declared him dead. Why they did that is yet another mystery. So, according to the first article, he was an old guy, a loner who was in the habit of fishing on the right bank, at the bend of the river before it reaches Saint-Pierre-des-Corps. You can't really see the spot from the highway."

"Think we should go find it for ourselves?"

"Yes, I do, son. But first I have to do that interview."

Thirty minutes later, Benjamin and Virgile were in the Mercedes again, driving to the fishing spot where Octave Pastier had disappeared. It was secluded and overgrown, much the way it was in the nineteen thirties, Benjamin surmised. They lingered there, envisioning the old man inspecting his line, baiting his hook, and looking for fish.

"I can see him now, boss. A hand-rolled cigarette hanging from his lips. Wearing an old pair of trousers, flannel shirt, and suspenders, his face bruised and battered with age, a snack in his bag."

Benjamin nodded as he looked down the river, his hand shielding his eyes from the sun. "Let's go back to Montlouis and find someone who can tell us about our Octave."

He had jotted down the names of the residents interviewed in the original article and hoped to locate a few of their relatives. Octave's housekeeper was one of the interviewees. She had lived in his rather large home, which was perched on a hill above town. They decided to make the former residence their first stop.

Arriving, they discovered that the place had been totally renovated and was now gated. Benjamin parked by the side of the road and got out. A white-haired man in a suit had emerged from the house and was heading toward a Citroën C4 Picasso in the driveway. Seeing Benjamin at the gate, he waved and walked over.

"Yes? Can I help you?" he asked.

"Please pardon the intrusion," Benjamin said. "I'm looking for relatives of Octave Pastier, who used to own this place, or his housekeeper. I'm wondering if you might be able to help."

The man scratched his head. "Pastier lived here a long time ago, and he was a bachelor. He didn't have any survivors to speak of, although I did hear that he had a relative in Vouvray. As for the housekeeper, she also died a long time ago. But I can put you in touch with her granddaughter. She's my contact at the catering company my architecture firm uses." He pulled out his phone and looked up her number, which he then gave to Benjamin.

"Thank you," Benjamin said. "You've been a great help." He walked back to the Mercedes and called the housekeeper's granddaughter, Denise Tolbert. They arranged to meet at a café.

The meeting with Denise Tolbert lasted well over an hour. It seemed that Octave's disappearance coincided with a dispute he was having with the relative in Vouvray—a cousin who owned a substantial estate.

"If I'm not mistaken, that estate's where the actor David Navarre lives now—the Tremblay place," Denise said, stirring sugar into her coffee.

Benjamin and Virgile looked at each other.

"You know him—the actor?" Denise asked.

"We're acquainted with him," Virgile answered. "So, can you tell us more about what happened to Octave?"

"One night he didn't return from fishing," Denise said. "No one was especially worried, as he sometimes stopped for a few drinks before going home. It was my grandmother who sounded the alarm. Actually, they were a little more than employer and employee, if you know what I mean."

Benjamin nodded. "Go on."

"You can imagine the uproar when everyone realized he'd disappeared. The locals organized a search for Octave, and his cousin was at the head of the pack. They went up the river in a boat, combed the smallest islets, and scoured the banks to the foot of the cliffs. Finally, they gave up and faced facts: Octave was gone. Either he lay at the bottom of the Loire, or the current had carried him much farther downstream. They decided he was dead."

Denise sipped her coffee. "I've told you quite a bit about Octave and my grandmother," she said, putting her cup down. "Now, can you tell me why you're so interested in them?"

"You deserve as much," Benjamin answered, motioning to the server for more tea. "David Navarre has asked us to investigate a discovery at his estate. A skeleton was found behind a wall in his wine cellar, and we believe it was Octave."

"No kidding," Denise said. "After all these years? How would it have gotten there?"

Benjamin stared at the steam rising from his tea, which had just arrived. "After taking in all this information, I may have a theory."

Virgile leaned in. "And it's…"

"It's a matter of time and place. First: Vouvray and Montlouis are separated by the Loire. But in the nineteen thirties, something else came between them. Vouvray and Montlouis were divided into two distinct wine-growing areas. Remember when I told you they were in the same district once? Vouvray became the first appellation of controlled origin in the Loire Valley, while Montlouis was considered something of a poor relative. That's not the case today, mind you. Montlouis is well respected for its wine. But being split up more than eighty years ago fueled a rivalry. According to some people, they keep a close eye on each other even now."

"And what does that have to do with Octave?" Virgile asked.

"It's possible that Octave's cousin, the estate owner in Vouvray and the old bachelor's sole heir, murdered Octave to get his hands on both the land in Montlouis and the hectares Octave owned in Vouvray, which, coincidentally, adjoined the Tremblay estate. Why hide the body in the cellar, you ask? In my opinion, he wanted to put him in a place where no one would go searching. Or rather, where no one would dare to, because the cellars around here are virtual sanctuaries. You don't go poking around in them."

"And the cousin was probably trying to avoid suspicion by heading the search party and pretending to be worried," Virgile said.

Benjamin looked at Denise. "Would you happen to know the exact location of the land in Vouvray?"

Denise shook her head. "That I can't tell you, but it would be easy enough to find the answer."

Benjamin finished his tea. "You've been quite helpful," he said. "And the next time you're in Bordeaux, please give us a call. Since you're in the catering business, you might be interested in seeing what we do."

"That's most kind of you, Mr. Cooker."

Benjamin picked up the check, ready to leave.

"It's too bad, though, what happened to the cousin."

Startled, Benjamin turned his attention from the check back to Denise. "Oh? What happened?"

"According to my grandmother, dead-arm disease hit the vines shortly after he inherited the land in Vouvray. None of the neighboring vineyards were affected. The vines died. Then he came down with a dental infection that spread to his brain. He lingered in acute pain for some time before passing away."

Benjamin tried to keep his jaw from dropping. "Thank you for that piece of information." He said a hurried good-bye and headed toward the café door, with Virgile close behind.

"I've got a bad feeling about this, boss. Where are we going now?"

"Back to the town hall in Vouvray."

Once there, they found the same clerk, Yvette.

"I'd like to see the property records for the Tremblay estate and the parcels adjoining it," Benjamin said. The winemaker combed through all of them until he found what he was looking for. "Just what I thought, Virgile."

Virgile leaned over his shoulder. "It's the same parcel that David wants us to revive." He pulled over a chair and sat down beside the winemaker. "Do you believe in jinxes, boss?"

18

Benjamin called David Navarre. He planned to share his news about Octave Pastier and his cousin, but not all of it right away. Two other matters had precedence. He needed to restore Virgile's reputation in David's eyes, and he intended to get the actor out of his château. David had been holed up there, knocking back tumblers of whiskey far too long. It was late in the afternoon, but they still had time to squeeze in a visit to Domaine Huet. Benjamin asked David to join them. He initially refused, offering a feeble excuse, but he finally relented.

Sitting on the hood of the convertible, Benjamin and Virgile waited for the actor. Less than a quarter of an hour later, David arrived on his motorcycle, sans helmet, jacket, and boots. Freshly shaved and in a black T-shirt and jeans, he looked younger than his age. Benjamin had to hand it to him. The man was still able to muster up the sense of ease and a way of winking at life that had made him so magnetic on screen. True, he had put on a few pounds, and his features had thickened, but there remained something intact in him: a permanent state of grace that allowed him to hold on and bounce back. It almost seemed that he could rise from the ashes.

"So, what's this news you have for me?" he asked, getting off his motorcycle.

"I think we may have solved your skeleton mystery," Benjamin said. "We have reason to believe it's the remains of the cousin of a former owner of your estate."

"Really?" David said. "Tell me more."

"You deserve the whole story, David, and we will share it with you, along with the police. The story also involves that parcel you want to revive."

"Now you'll have me stewing, Benjamin. Must I wait?"

"Not to worry, David. We'll sort through everything. But I also asked you here to give my assistant a chance to talk with you himself."

Benjamin turned to Virgile, who cleared his throat.

"Mr. Navarre, I'm so sorry about what happened. I never could have guessed that a simple dance would have such repercussions."

Virgile's apprehension was written all over his face. That David did his own fight scenes was well known. And despite his hallmark charm, he could nurse a grudge. Benjamin braced himself to intervene. But instead of turning red-faced and balling up his fists, the actor grinned.

"Okay, don't worry, kid. I got it. I'm sorry the cops screwed you like a rookie. I hope you do better in the wine cellars. From what your boss tells me, you're the man."

"That's where I'm on safe ground, although you could say there's always a tremor or two in the wine industry."

"Virgile and I work as a team," Benjamin said. "When you hire Cooker & Co., you hire both of us."

"Understood," David said, shaking Virgile's hand.

Benjamin smiled, relieved that relations were finally restored. As the three men walked toward the office, a man in a zip-up cardigan, plaid shirt, and jeans came out to greet them.

"Gentlemen, welcome to Domaine Huet. I'm Pierre. Jean-Bernard Berthome, our cellar master, extends his apologies. He was called away."

"It's we who should apologize for giving you such short notice," Benjamin said. "My assistant,

Virgile, and I are in the area to film a documentary, and I just couldn't leave without squeezing in a visit. This is Virgile's first time. And we asked Mr. Navarre to join us."

"Good to see you again," David said, shaking Pierre's hand. "Benjamin, I've been here many times. You could call us neighbors."

"Yes, we've been following Mr. Navarre's work at his estate with great interest," Pierre said. He looked over Benjamin's shoulder. "But you mentioned a documentary? I don't see anyone with cameras or microphones."

"We've just stopped by to say a friendly hello," Benjamin said. "I have no intention of taking out my notebook or evaluating your latest vintages. We've come to bother you as simple tourists."

"I'm sure Mr. Berthome will appreciate that." This was said tongue-in-cheek. Domaine Huet had never complained about its ratings in the *Cooker Guide*.

The thirty-five-hectare Huet estate, established in 1928 by Victor Huet, comprised three properties: La Haut-Lieu, Le Mont, and Le Clos du Bourg. In 1971, Noel Pinguet, the son-in-law of second-generation owner Gaston Huet, joined the estate. Together, Gaston and Noel crafted legendary wines for more than three decades.

When Gaston fell ill in 2002, a search for a business partner who could ensure the estate's legacy was launched, and New York financier Anthony Hwang was brought in. After Gaston's death that year, daily operations were handed over to Pinguet.

Pinguet, the mathematician son of a butcher, became the face of the domain. He was called meticulous—even maniacal—insisting on farming without chemicals and following the phases of the moon.

Pinguet and Hwang worked together for ten years, until Pinguet's 2012 retirement three years earlier than planned. Members of the Hwang family were reportedly pressuring Pinguet to produce more dry wines than he wanted, a claim the Hwang family denied.

After Pinguet's departure, the winemaking and vineyard duties were transferred to Berthome, who had worked at the estate, focusing mainly on the vineyards, for more than thirty years. His vintages were known for their purity and consistency, and Benjamin considered himself a great admirer.

Pierre nodded toward the cellar. "Follow me," he said. "We'll go treasure hunting."

Pierre proceeded to guide them through an impressive rock labyrinth, kilometers of tunnels carved under the vines. They came upon long corridors bathed in soft light, crypts with high ceilings, narrow passageways, caves holding old bottles, steep staircases difficult to descend, other precipitous staircases even more challenging to climb, and many wide, damp corridors where a person could get lost, even disappear. Thousands of bottles, all carefully stored, were waiting to be exhumed and brought to the light of day.

Both Pierre and David provided a narrative as they moved along, with Pierre stopping occasionally to examine a bottle or recall a harvest memory.

"They've upheld the tradition of biodynamic farming—a return to the understanding of nature that farmers had before technology came along," David said.

Pierre continued. "By attempting to modify everything, we often sever our connection to the earth. Here, we apply copper and sulfate in homeopathic doses and only when necessary. We have the hindsight to know that with biodynamic farming, the risk of vine disease is minimal."

They reached a vaulted room with columns where the wine presses were once housed. Only the hollowed-out rock with angular friezes remained. Benjamin had the feeling he was visiting an Etruscan tomb.

"I guess we could call it 'archoenology,'" Virgile joked.

Pierre looked over at David. "Perhaps if we did some digging, we'd find a skeleton here, as well."

David grunted. "I wouldn't wish that on you, my friend."

The group emerged from the cellar and headed for the owner's house, perched on a plateau at the end of a long dirt road. From the terrace, the panoramic view of the Loire Valley was magnificent. The men collapsed on teak garden chairs.

Just as Pierre was opening a bottle of Cuvée Constance Moelleux, 2005, David's cell phone rang.

"It's Molinier," he said, looking at the screen. "I have to take this."

David walked away, and Benjamin, Virgile, and Pierre waited. A few minutes later, he returned, smiling. "Good news, gentlemen. Simone is stirring."

"That's wonderful," Benjamin said. "Does it mean she's coming out of her coma?"

"Too soon to tell, but she could be."

"I'm truly happy for you, Mr. Navarre," Virgile said.

"Molinier warned that we shouldn't get ahead of ourselves. Even if she emerges completely from her coma, she'll have a long row to hoe."

"I propose that we drink to Simone's improved condition," Benjamin said. "And there's no better wine for that than the one we have here."

Pierre poured the Cuvée Constance Moelleux.

Benjamin turned to Virgile. "What you're looking at, son, is the crown jewel of this estate's production. It's named after Gaston Huet's mother, Constance. It's intense and pure. Some even call it ethereal. The grapes are painstakingly selected, one by one, in the perfect state of noble rot."

Virgile held the transparent sweet wine up to his eyes before plunging his nose into the glass and sniffing. Finally, he tasted it.

Benjamin waited.

"Quince jelly, lemon candy, marzipan, heliotrope, grapefruit, and honey," Virgile said, looking up. "It's incredibly light, despite the richness of the honey."

"I'm astounded you found all those words, Virgile. This wine leaves some people speechless."

Pierre set a mahogany cigar box down on the table, and Benjamin chose a Punch Royal Selection. Lighting up, he savored the earthy blend of black cherry and chocolate. "You should never resist the instinctive search for contentment," he murmured. "I don't remember who said, 'The best cigar in the world is the one you prefer to smoke on special occasions, enabling you to relax and enjoy that which gives you maximum pleasure.'"

"You're sure you don't know who said that, boss?"

Benjamin glanced at his assistant, catching his drift. "I think it was Zino Davidoff."

"You think, or you're sure?"

"Go check for yourself, son."

19

Château de Pray was peaceful. After a copious dinner, Benjamin and Virgile went out to the terrace for their liqueurs.

They had spoken little while eating. Virgile, voracious and oblivious to propriety, had buried his nose in his dish. He was clearly focused on making up the calories lost during his custody. The Touraine was certainly a land of contrasts. Between Inspector Blanchet's urine-soaked cell and the fashionable décor of Château de Pray was an abyss the young man crossed without qualms.

Leaving Domaine Huet that afternoon, Benjamin had pulled David aside and shared the rest of what he had learned about Octave Pastier and the former owner of the Tremblay estate. David, bolstered by the news about Simone, had seemed stable enough by the end of the visit to handle it.

He was wrong. David was taken aback. "If I didn't know better, I'd say the place is cursed,

Benjamin. Is it possible that no vines will grow on that soil?"

"I'm not a superstitious man," Benjamin had said. "I'm a scientist. We'll do a thorough analysis. I'm sure any vestiges of black-arm disease are gone. Don't worry, David. We'll take care of it."

Benjamin was still recalling the conversation when they arrived on the terrace and found Lee Friedman, in sneakers and a Les Bleus baseball cap, seated under the glow of a wrought-iron lamp. Surrounded by piles of scribbled papers, he was working on his laptop.

"Good evening, gentlemen!" Lee said. "Come join me in the cool night air."

"You look so studious, we wouldn't want to disturb you," Benjamin responded. Despite Lee's hearty greeting, he couldn't miss the circles under his eyes and the tight jaw muscles.

"No disturbance at all," Lee said, pulling two chairs closer to his table. "I was just working on a rough draft of a new screenplay."

"Already?" Benjamin asked. "When you haven't signed the contract for your project with Gayraud?"

"A writer's always thinking of stories, Benjamin. Besides, sometimes it's the only way to get your mind off your worries, if you know what I mean."

Benjamin didn't answer and sat down.

"So, have you thanked our chef for his works of art?" Lee asked. "What am I saying? For his masterpieces!"

Virgile patted his stomach. His color had returned, and there was a twinkle in his eye. "For starters, I had pine nut and roquette salad. Then I ordered the blue lobster with morels, followed by a cheese platter and crispy grapes covered with foam and grape leaves."

"Very good choices, each one," Lee said. "What about you, Benjamin?"

"I wasn't very hungry when we ordered. But the more I watched Virgile eat, the more gluttonous I became. It was contagious, like yawning."

"The important thing is to enjoy yourself without remorse," Lee said.

"Oh, you can count on me to enjoy myself," Benjamin said. "Still, I didn't intend to indulge that way."

"In your defense, you didn't take any cheese," Virgile said. "What's more, in this rare instance, we drank only one bottle of wine: a dry Montlouis from François Chidaine."

"It was perfection," Benjamin enthused. "Layered with complex fruit and charged with vivacious minerality. If we have enough time, we'll visit François with the film crew. He's a winemaker who pays attention to detail, and, Virgile, I'd like you to watch him up close. He makes his own organic sprays. For him, biodynamic methods are a religion, and his approach is impeccable. He believes in very low yields. In the cellar, he takes great care with his pressings, and he uses only wild yeast…"

Lee sighed. "You make him sound like a zealot, Benjamin. There's nothing extremist about him. I happen to think he's a reasonable man."

"You're absolutely right, Lee," the winemaker replied with a smile. "Rigor's an essential component of reasoned viticulture." He turned back to Virgile. "Unfortunately, we've lost a day, and I don't think we'll be able to squeeze in Jacky Blot at his Taille aux Loups estate. He has a different style, another way of caring for his chenin grapes. He's more sophisticated in his presentation. I remember a 2001 Rémus that was very balanced and elegant. I also like his Vouvray and Bourgueil. What an intense taste of fruit!"

Lee closed his laptop. "I don't know how you handle so many tastings, Benjamin. It's a hell of a lot of work and requires an enormous amount of concentration."

"It's all in the discipline. Ironically, it's in the passion, as well. 'Too much and too little wine. Give him none, he cannot find truth; give him too much, the same.' Blaise Pascal."

"So that's the secret." Lee said. "Tell me, Benjamin. I hear Gayraud's found a solution to his problem and won't have to delay filming the movie. They're replacing Simone."

"That's not definite, at this point, at least. Dr. Molinier thinks Simone may be coming out of her coma."

"Now that's good news! David must be heartened."

"I think he's feeling better. But we still don't know if she'll recover fully and resume filming. I'm sure they'll secure this new actress as a backup. I've seen her, and I think she'd do well."

"Where was this?"

"Well, I didn't see her in the flesh. I just helped in the selection. I was with David when Gayraud showed up with a binder. She was the clear choice."

"But is this girl as good as Simone?"

"I can't tell you. I only saw her photo and bio. But she appears to be completely charming. She has a little mole close to her lip that reminds me of a famous model. She has long auburn hair. I forget her name, but you know who I mean."

"Cindy Crawford, boss."

"Of course, you'd know her name." If only Virgile could so easily remember every beautiful wine he'd ever tasted.

"Well, she has been around for a while," Virgile said. "And there aren't that many actresses or models with moles close to their lips."

"I suppose." Benjamin wanted to backtrack. "Lee, you're familiar with mysteries. Do you have a theory on what happened to Simone?"

"No, not really," Lee said. "If she never recovers, that's too bad, but you know as well as I do that starlets come and go."

Benjamin saw Virgile stiffen at the insensitivity.

Immediately, Lee tried to soften his words. "To be honest, I haven't thought about Simone that much. You do have to wonder about the GHB. Who'd have the stuff, and did the perpetrator use it to rape her or kill her—or both?"

Benjamin and Virgile exchanged a glance.

"It seems you know more about it than I do," Lee said.

"Not really," Benjamin answered. "I was also at the château when Dr. Molinier told David about the GHB. How did you know?"

"Simone's a celebrity. Where there's a celebrity, there're leaks."

Benjamin waited for Lee to divulge more about his source, but he didn't.

"Obviously, the police are taking the GHB connection seriously," Lee said. "Otherwise they would have gone with alcohol-induced coma. That would have made it simple: she drank too much. Case closed."

"I didn't even know there was such a drug before this happened," Benjamin said.

Lee shrugged. "You can find it at any night spot. Guys are out on the hunt. They figure, 'Why spend all your money and energy on seducing a girl, when you can plop something in her drink, take her into a back room or her apartment, and be done with it.' Not that I approve, mind you. But I'm not surprised that someone—or more than one person—would have been using it at the party that night. All you had to do was look around, and you could see that half of them were wasted."

"So, as far as you're concerned, who are the main suspects?" Virgile asked.

"Everyone's presumed guilty—even the host himself," Lee said.

"But Simone's his girlfriend. Why would he slip GHB into her drink?"

"Who knows? Maybe he wanted her to enjoy herself, and considering what happened, he doesn't have the guts to fess up. Then again, he's a man with a big ego. Perhaps he saw Simone flirting with you and wanted to hurt her."

"Could he have been that angry—so angry he'd drug and rape her—or, even worse, allow someone else to assault her?" Virgile asked. "You'd have to be a despicable person to do something like that."

"Men who've claimed to love the women in their lives have done terrible things," Lee answered. "Men you'd like if you met them in a café."

"Who else could have done it?" Benjamin asked.

"It could have been anyone, I tell you."

"Jean-Paul Gayraud?"

"Why not? He's capable of anything, especially if it benefits his wallet. But he's a harder person to pin it on. I can't see why he'd kill the goose that laid one of his golden eggs. Besides, he left early that night."

"So then, who else?"

"You... Me... Who knows? Maybe an envious woman, a vengeful ex-lover, a rejected suitor. A stage hand or a makeup artist who's been mistreated. A nasty journalist. A bitter director. Hasn't it ever crossed your mind to bump someone off?"

Benjamin leaned back and folded his arms. "But was this a murder attempt or a sexual assault with life-threatening consequences? Or could it have been an innocent mistake?"

Lee seemed fatigued. He reached into a back pocket of his jeans and pulled out a small round box. He opened it and took out two capsules, which he swallowed with the remaining drops of his Armagnac. Benjamin watched and waited.

"Attempted murder is certainly a possibility," Lee said. "But you can't deny there are more tried-and-true methods if you absolutely want to bump someone off. I understand what you're getting at, Benjamin, and it's an important point. In the case of Simone Margerolle, it's difficult to tease out the real intentions of the perpetrator. But we must remember that the dose was probably very high, since she's been in a coma, and for that reason, I don't think it was an innocent mistake."

"I think this real-life mystery has the makings of a first-rate screenplay," Benjamin said. "Just consider the number of suspects. And with all the possible perpetrators you've ticked off, you haven't even mentioned someone who, for all intents and purposes, didn't even know her before the night of David's party."

"If that's the case, someone else will have to write it," Lee said. "Not me. I'm in the mood for something more escapist."

"That's your right," Benjamin said. "Sometimes I turn down collaborations with property owners I don't much care for or terroirs that don't interest me. I'd never produce a wine that I've no desire to drink."

The men fell silent. Moments later, Virgile sighed and got up. "Boss, it's been a long day, and I want to catch up on some of the shut-eye I lost while I was Inspector Blanchet's guest. The accommodations weren't exactly conducive to sleep."

"Go ahead, Virgile. We have a busy day tomorrow. I'll spend a few more minutes down here."

Benjamin waited until Virgile was back in the château before saying anything. "Forgive me for prying, Lee, but I'm concerned. You told me about your troubles, and you aren't looking well. I also see that you're on medication."

"I'm fine, Benjamin. Really. I'm working with a new therapist, and he prescribed a different anti-depressant. My old one wasn't working." Lee looked at his watch. "Well, it's past midnight already. I should hit the sack too."

As he started gathering up everything, he pulled out the round pill box from beneath his papers. "I almost forgot this. I didn't even close the lid."

Lee placed the papers in a cardboard folder. He capped his pen and picked up a paperback opened to a page with paragraphs highlighted in pink. "A few pages of reading to maintain my form, and then it's nighty-night." Covering his mouth, he yawned.

"Balzac." Benjamin said, tilting his head to read the title. "*A Woman of Thirty*. I love that novel."

"So do I. I bought it for my visit here. He writes about this area. There are some beautiful passages, especially this one about Château de Moncontour. Did you know Balzac wanted to live in Vouvray?"

"Yes, so it seems."

"Listen to this: 'Moncontour is an old manor house built upon the sandy cliffs situated on one of those white rocks above the Loire… It is a picturesque white château, with turrets covered with fine stone carving like Mechlin lace; a château such as you often see in Touraine, spick and span, ivy-clad, standing among its groves of mulberry-trees and vineyards, with its sunken paths, its openwork balustrades, and cellars mined in the rock escarpments mirrored in the Loire. The roofs of Moncontour glisten under the sun's rays.' And then, further on, at the bottom of the page, there are some phrases that I find still true: 'a fair, sweet-scented country, where pain is lulled to sleep and passion wakes. No heart is cold for long beneath its clear sky, beside its sparkling waters. One ambition dies after another, and you sink into serene content and repose, as the sun sinks at the end of the day swathed about with purple and azure.'"

"Very true," Benjamin said. "There's something in the air that rocks and soothes you."

"That's how Balzac writes about Vouvray. I've bookmarked a passage: a letter to Countess Hanska, dated June 10, 1846: 'Moncontour is my predilection, I'd like you to come and see it, it is so lovely. It's one of the most beautiful views of the Touraine.' He was born in Touraine, and he hoped to acquire the château. But he never had the money. I'm afraid that's also my fate. I'll have nothing left after I pay off my wife and lawyer. That's if Gayraud coughs up what he owes me."

"I'd say hitch your wagon to another producer the next time around."

"Sage advice, Benjamin."

The two men parted ways, with Benjamin shaking Lee's hand. As soon as Lee was out of sight, Benjamin opened his left hand and slipped the capsule that had fallen out of the pill box into his pocket.

20

"The sound of the waters lapping in the Loire will add some ambiance, I think." Liza Stechelmann scanned the river and the gently rising banks lined with trees, which were flaunting their leaves in full springtime splendor. She looked back at Benjamin and Virgile, waiting for confirmation.

"Yes, I agree," Virgile said. "I've always loved the sound of water. I belonged to the Bergerac rowing club when I was a kid."

"Is that so?"

"It's true," Benjamin said. "He was one of its most promising members."

The production team had borrowed a boat, and they were steadying it so the winemaker and his assistant could get in. Liza had equipped the two oenologists with clip-on microphones. Fabrice would stretch out on the bank and follow them with his camera.

"I'm miking you, but I probably won't use anything you say," Liza said. "These are just atmospheric images to mark breaks in the action. Feel free to say whatever."

Virgile turned to Benjamin. "I wonder if it's okay to swim here. I wouldn't mind jumping in after the filming."

"I wouldn't know, son. The Loire's been called the last wild river in Western Europe. It's a haven for rare and threatened wildlife. But it can also have high levels of algae and bacteria. I wouldn't swim in it."

"You really think it's that big a concern?"

"I wouldn't take a chance. Some of the river's more popular swimming spots were closed last year."

"But that was in the summer, boss."

"Correct. So you decide for yourself."

Benjamin leaned over side of the boat and stared at the water. It was bringing back memories of his childhood: August, when his family vacationed in the Médoc, and the sun would darken freckles faded by overcast winters in London. Back then, the Médoc's famous wine estates—Margaux, Latour, Petrus, and Mouton-Rothschild, to name a few—didn't interest him the way they would later. When his father, Paul William, drove them to the ocean, Benjamin couldn't wait for the familiar curves in the road announcing the promise of a swim.

Paul William shunned the water himself, but he allowed his children to frolic in the waves. While Benjamin's mother read magazines and sunbathed, without undressing too much, Paul William would watch his children with the austere dignity of an officer in the Royal Navy—taking care to keep his deerskin Lobbs dry. Much earlier, he had advised Benjamin and his siblings to watch out for eddies and shifting sand banks, as the currents were often treacherous.

Liza interrupted his reverie. "Would you please make a U-turn, but not too quickly," she yelled from the river bank. Apparently, she wanted to get the bridge in the background.

"I'd like to see you do this!" Virgile called out. "You're making me row against the current!"

"Put in the effort, please," the director yelled back, cupping her hands around her mouth like a megaphone.

"My hands are already blistered. I'm out of practice."

"Come, come, Virgile. Don't be a sissy!"

Liza's words stung. Virgile heaved and executed the maneuver without a word.

Benjamin, meanwhile, had closed his eyes and was letting the gentle waters lull him. His young gondolier was seething and chastising himself for going along with this little boat trip, and the winemaker wasn't about to get in the middle of it.

$\mathcal{S} \ \mathcal{S} \ \mathcal{S}$

Still muttering, Virgile climbed out of the boat and let Benjamin huddle with Liza. They walked over to a cluster of trees and didn't seem to notice that he wasn't following. Instead, Virgile stayed where he was and watched as Fabrice dusted the dirt and grass off his jeans and polo shirt and changed lenses. Then, as if sensing that he was being studied, he looked up from his camera and locked eyes with Virgile.

Virgile didn't want to wait any longer. He climbed the river bank and joined Fabrice.

"I think we're almost done with the filming phase of the documentary," he said, attempting a casual conversation as he stood shoulder-to-shoulder with the cameraman. "Will you be glad to get back to Paris?"

"No, not really," Fabrice said. "The country-side's nice, and the pay's okay. As long as I can get my workouts in, I'm good."

"So, is it hard to stay in shape while you're traveling?"

Fabrice looked over at him. "I learned a long time ago that the secret's bringing your own equipment. I've got a suspension trainer, a speed rope, resistance bands, an ab wheel... I even have a medicine ball you fill with water when you use it and drain when you're done. And I eat right. I pack a lot of my own food."

Virgile put his hands in his pockets and fell silent for a moment. Then: "Just wondering—do you ever compete in bodybuilding contests?"

Fabrice's expression turned curious. "It's not my thing. I care about staying fit, but I'm not someone's eye candy. And so many bodybuilders in those competitions take enhancers. I don't. Why are you asking?"

Virgile had a gut feeling. The guy was telling the truth. He took a deep breath and plunged in. "I've got to ask, Fabrice. I was at the hospital the day after Simone was admitted. The nurse told me you visited her too."

Fabrice looked shocked. "How did she know it was me? I didn't give her my name."

"You didn't have to give her your name. You're someone who stands out in a crowd."

Fabrice sighed and hung his head. "Yeah, I was at the hospital. I had to see her. After we finished filming at the party, David said we could stay. I packed my gear and just starting mingling. Then she came up and asked me to dance. Virgile, it was a dance I'll remember the rest of my life. A gorgeous girl like her, looking at me that way, like I was the only man in the world. I was walking on air. Then, before I knew it, she vanished. The next morning, they told me she'd been found unconscious in the cellar. I couldn't believe it." The cameraman kicked the dirt. "So that's why I was at the hospital. I really hope, by some miracle, that she recovers. I've been praying for her."

Virgile understood. "I know, Fabrice. I hope she recovers too." He patted the cameraman's shoulder.

"Tell me, why were you at the hospital?" Fabrice asked.

"You're not the only one who danced with Simone, remember? I'm sure you saw the photo in the magazine. It was enough to have me held at police headquarters. Simone pulled a vanishing act on me that night, the same way she did with you. She's magic, that's for sure."

The two men exchanged a smile.

"All right," Virgile said after a moment. "I think it's time to join the others."

Virgile and Fabrice headed over to Benjamin, Liza, and Hugo. The director and her team got into their van, and the winemaker and his assistant climbed into the Mercedes.

"I saw you talking with Fabrice," Benjamin said. "Did you get anything?"

"Yeah, boss, I did. He's an ordinary guy like me. One dance, and he's swept off his feet."

"Well, I just picked up a piece of information, Virgile. Liza told me she spotted a man coming on to Simone in a dimly lit corner of the château the night of David's party. He was all over Simone, and she wasn't having it. She shoved him—hard. When he turned around, all red-faced, Liza recognized him. She'd seen him talking with the two of us and Gayraud earlier."

"How does she know Gayraud?"

"He's one of the biggest movie producers in France, son. He's been photographed hundreds of times."

"Then there's only one other person it could have been."

"Right. Lee Friedman. Rumor has it David bedded Lee's wife awhile ago."

"So maybe he was trying to even the score?"

"Could be. Imagine the humiliation of Simone's rejection, especially if he'd seen her coming on to you and then Fabrice. It's possible he resorted to drugging Simone to have his way with her."

Virgile shook his head. "I don't want to think about it, boss. I like Lee. He's cynical, yes. But really, he's just a sad sack. I can't picture him as a rapist."

"It's hard for me to see him that way too. Still, I can't dismiss Lee as a suspect. I managed to pocket a bit of evidence the other night. It'll either clear him or convict him."

21

Benjamin and Virgile gave the next three days to Liza, who was tying up the project. What she seemed most interested in having them do was traipse through the vineyards while discussing their calling. She would intersperse the tasting sessions with these moments.

"I feel like I'm running a marathon," Virgile said, mopping his forehead as they left yet another estate on an unusually warm afternoon.

Benjamin nodded. He was growing weary too.

The documentary's sequence seemed already planned out, but Liza wouldn't divulge it. "I have an inkling," she would joke when Benjamin or Virgile questioned why she was taking one shot or another.

The two wine experts discussed whatever came to mind, according to their mood and the particular stroll through the vines, as was their routine at other estates when they weren't being filmed.

One of their favorite topics: the astonishing range of Loire appellations. Benjamin listed in rapid succession the most important of the terroirs, from the schistose terrain of Anjou to the sandy soil of Sologne. He pointed out their distinctive qualities, the vegetation, the richness of micro-expressions, the under-recognized vineyards, and much more. For his part, Virgile asked falsely naïve questions so that Benjamin could educate the viewers.

"Excellent, gentlemen!" Liza shouted at the end of each segment.

Their last scheduled visit was at the estate owned by Philippe Foreau, a third-generation winemaker. With twelve hectares divided into twenty parcels, Le Close Naudin had established itself among the Vouvray wines prized beyond the borders of France. Liza, fearing she might have too much footage, didn't want to dawdle here. But Benjamin had no intention of skipping over this passionate yet low-profile winemaker and depriving himself of his outstanding offerings, especially the prized 2015 vintages, which Philippe had declared perhaps the finest of his lifetime.

"As you remember, Virgile, the summer in this region was dry and warm," Benjamin said as

Philippe led them to a long wooden table where they would be tasting. "I understand the vineyards needed only four treatments, and you picked the grapes at their prime. Is that correct, Philippe?"

Philippe nodded and poured a sec for Benjamin and Virgile. The winemaker noted its bold personality and strong mineral backbone.

"I look forward to drinking this in six years," Benjamin said. "As good as it is now, it'll only get better."

Next, Benjamin and Virgile tasted a moelleux, which had a dense, almost bitter, aroma and notes of pear, pitted fruits, and honey.

"On the palate, the fruit is warm and leans toward quince and plum," Benjamin said. "But there's a spicy undercurrent, too. The finish is surprisingly dry."

Benjamin was set to taste more of the superb 2015 vintages, but Liza cut him short. "We've got what we need, she said, motioning to Fabrice and Hugo to pack up. I'm driving to Paris this evening to start going over the footage. You'll have to make time in your schedule for us to meet in Bordeaux. I plan to film you in your office and your laboratory, working with your technicians, and also at your home."

This was one edict too many for Benjamin, who wasn't going to the trouble of hiding his annoyance. "Oh, no, not Grangebelle," he said. "No filming of Saint-Julien-Beychevelle. It's private domain."

"We've been working together for a while now, Benjamin. You know I'm discreet."

"No, I said. My home and family are off limits."

Liza sighed. "All right, I won't insist. We'll start the documentary with just you in your office and lab, although I suppose we can get some shots in Bordeaux to add flavor."

"You shoot the beginning of the film at the end?" Virgile asked.

"That's often the case. The editing is the most important part. I've collected an enormous amount of footage, and the editing will take a long time. I'd like to have your approval on some of the scenes, Benjamin."

"I appreciate the gesture."

"It's professional courtesy, and besides, I prefer to avoid disagreements with you." For the first time since meeting him, Liza gave Benjamin an amused look, and he swore she winked at him. Benjamin couldn't help feeling exposed as a curmudgeon but admired nevertheless. He returned the conspiratorial smile and loosened up a bit before pulling out his notebook and pen. "When may I have a look at the first rushes?"

"I'll be working on the footage all week and through the weekend. If you could come to Paris next Monday, that would be perfect."

"Why not? We're not far from the capital. How long will it take to see everything?"

"You'll be viewing only what I'm keeping. I'd say we can get through it in one morning."

"So much the better. We'll drive back to Bordeaux at the end of the day."

Before telling them they could return to Château de Pray, Liza made one last request. She wanted a backlit shot of Benjamin and Virgile at the edge of the river, near the Amboise bridge. Liza and Fabrice stood a hundred meters away, filming the two silhouettes against the shimmering water, now rosy in the light of the setting sun. It was a melancholy moment for Benjamin. Despite the way Liza's expectations had chafed at him, he had formed a bond with the director and her assistants.

He was reflecting on how he would remember this time, when an abrupt noise startled him. "Did you hear that, Virgile?" he whispered.

"Yes, boss!"

"Don't turn around, son."

"Why?"

"I heard that sound the other day."

"When was that?"

"As I was leaving David's estate."

They pricked their ears. Click… Click… The same clipped metallic sound.

"I swear somebody's cocking a gun, Virgile." Benjamin's neck was prickling.

Virgile looked over and grinned. "It's obvious you've never been a hunter."

"What is it, then?"

"As Liza would say, I have an inkling."

With that, Virgile took off toward an overgrown area downstream. He reached the spot and dived into the foliage. Benjamin watched as the weeds and bushes shook. Above the sound of cracking branches, he heard a man yell and then cry out in pain. Holding his bloody nose, the stranger sprang from the shrubs and dashed away. Virgile emerged seconds later, wearing a triumphant grin. He waved a camera like a trophy, its zoom lens covered with mud.

"I clocked him, that stupid paparazzi," Virgile said. "I bet he's been following us for days. You can thank me, boss. I saved you from being on the cover of *Voici!*. I can picture the headline: "The famous winemaker's young lover.' Mrs. Cooker would have had a hard time explaining that."

Benjamin chuckled as his assistant checked his shirt for stray twigs and grass. "I think this is one time Elisabeth would have quoted Oscar Wilde herself."

"Oh? What quote is that, boss?"

"'I never take notice of what common people say.'"

22

David Navarre was curled on the floor like a fetus. Crouched beside him, Dr. Molinier was trying to console the actor with tissues, a glass of water, even whiskey.

"David, you must be strong," Molinier said softly as he stroked the sobbing man's hair. He had come to the estate to deliver the news: Simone had died at six fifty-three that morning. Her body was lying in the basement of the Institut médico-légal, in locker No. 7, waiting for someone to claim it.

The sight didn't surprise Benjamin. David, the likable yet self-absorbed actor, hadn't gathered the courage to go to his lover's bedside. For most of her absence, he had chosen to stay at the estate and drink himself senseless. Now that Simone was gone, he was writhing on the floor, cursing himself.

"She was getting better! How could she leave me this way?" Tears streamed down David's face. "I should have been there! And I should have stopped that bastard director. I let her down when I should have been by her side through everything."

Benjamin walked over to the two men and put his hand on the doctor's shoulder. The touch startled Molinier.

"Oh, Mr. Cooker, thank you for coming so quickly."

"What happened?" Benjamin asked. "I thought Simone was coming out of her coma."

"She was. But then she went into respiratory arrest. They did everything, but they couldn't revive her."

What a tragedy. Benjamin thought. He felt a wave of compassion for David. He had failed Simone. Still, he had loved her.

"He's drunk," the doctor said. "Would you help me get him on the couch?"

Benjamin and Molinier tried twice to pick up the actor, but hoisting eighty-two kilos of limp despair was nearly impossible.

David howled and curled up on the floor again. "I should have confronted that SOB Armond. Simone was right for wanting to sue the weasel. We would have sucked every euro out of him!" Then, a moment later: "She's a bitch for leaving me! I don't deserve it!"

"I just gave him an injection. It should take effect pretty soon," Molinier said.

Benjamin crouched alongside Molinier, who was stroking the actor's hair again.

"Sleep, David, sleep."

A few minutes later, he was babbling. The winemaker and the doctor waited a moment longer.

"There, he's asleep," Molinier murmured, rising to his feet.

"Will there be an autopsy?" Benjamin asked.

"At present, I can't tell you. She was teetering between life and death for some time, and in cases such as this one, a reversal isn't uncommon. I'll know more after I speak with her attending."

Benjamin nodded. "If there's an autopsy, please forward the results."

"I'll see what I can do," the doctor answered, tucking a pillow under David's head "We did get the results of the rape kit. Simone wasn't sexually assaulted. Maybe when David's calmer, he'll take comfort in that."

"But now homicide appears to be the more likely intent, although we can't rule out a thwarted rape. David won't take any comfort in that."

"You have a point."

The two men watched silently as David's chest rose and fell with each breath. He was snoring.

Benjamin turned back to Molinier. "I have another request. Could you have this analyzed and tell me what it is?" He handed over Lee's capsule.

Molinier examined it. "I can't tell by looking at it. May I ask why you want it analyzed?"

"Let's just say I'm curious."

The doctor slipped the capsule into the right pocket of his jacket. Molinier looked back at David and shook his head. "I had no choice but to come and tell him about Simone. I tried to break it to him gently, but he had already drunk a bottle of whiskey."

"There's no reason for you to blame yourself, doctor. Moments like this are extremely difficult, especially after your hopes have been raised."

"At least I could tell him she died quietly, Mr. Cooker. There was no need to use a defibrillator. It's often a lifesaving piece of equipment, but it's violent. Simone just stopped breathing and slipped away." Molinier pulled a handkerchief out of his pocket and dabbed his eyes.

"Here one moment, gone the next," Benjamin thought as he watched the doctor fold his handkerchief and put it back in his pocket. "Not unlike the way she lived."

23

Benjamin took his time driving back to Château de Pray. He wasn't looking forward to breaking the news to Virgile. Oddly, he was thinking of Margaux, too. She had so much ahead of her, but life could be precarious. Nothing was a given. God forbid that anything should happen to her.

And what about this new person whose photo she'd posted on Instagram? He talked with Margaux regularly, but she hadn't mentioned him. Usually, they discussed his work or her work. Benjamin shook his head. He had gotten lazy. He and Margaux loved each other. Of this he was sure. But he wanted a deeper relationship, one in which she felt free to tell him anything, within reason, of course. He'd call her later that evening.

He found Virgile in his room and invited him to the little salon for a drink. "I know it's early, but I could use one."

"Sure, boss," Virgile said, studying his face. "You look down in the dumps. What happened?"

"I'll tell you when we get there, son."

The winemaker and his assistant walked down the stairs and seated themselves. Benjamin ordered their drinks and turned to Virgile. He didn't mince his words.

"I just came from David's estate. Simone is gone."

Virgile slumped in his chair. Benjamin waited for him to get his bearings.

"I'd allowed myself to think she could recover," Virgile said finally. "I knew it was a long shot, but still… What happened?"

"She stopped breathing. They couldn't revive her."

"When did she die?"

"This morning, very early."

Virgile wiped his face. "David must be devastated."

"You could say that. He was drunk, and then Dr. Molinier administered some sedation. He'll be numb for a while."

A server brought their drinks, Château de Prada once again. Benjamin took a whiff. The sweet burn of the aftertaste felt good.

"So, what do you think?" Virgile asked.

"I think we have some suspects, but all the pieces haven't fallen into place. The authorities haven't decided on an autopsy. If they go ahead, I want the results. We do have the findings of the rape-kit exam, and according to them, Simone wasn't sexually assaulted. That would appear to eliminate Fabrice. I know you believed his story."

"I admit I'm relieved, boss. I like the guy. But I have to ask: what about David? I know he loved Simone, but he doesn't seem to be that balanced a guy."

Benjamin took another sip of his Cognac and slowly put his glass down.

"Yes, despite his charm and casual demeanor, he can be suspicious, insecure, and mercurial. Simone was young and beautiful, while he's beginning to show his age. Her flirtations had to get under his skin."

"In addition, he's an actor," Virgile said. "He could easily put on a big show of innocence and grief."

"That's true." Benjamin fell silent for a moment. "But I have a gut feeling about David, something like the feeling you have about Fabrice. I don't think he did it. I've known David for some time. He can lose his temper, but he's not capable of premeditated murder."

"And that would leave… Who, boss?"

"David muttered something when I was at the estate, something about legal action against Max Armond, who was directing the film Simone and David were in."

"I've heard rumors about that guy. Apparently, he can make life hell for young actresses. Was Simone about to sue him for sexual harassment?"

"I don't know, but it's possible, and we did see him the night of the party. I'm sure a man with his connections has access to GHB. What's more, he had opportunity. But there's someone else, Virgile."

"Who's that?"

"Lee Friedman, remember? David had sex with his wife, and then, when Lee tried to get back at him by coming on to Simone, she rejected him."

"I'm sure that felt like a kick in the gut."

Benjamin shifted in his chair. "Clearly, Lee's not doing well. He's taking an anti-depressant. He said it's a new one."

"I hope it works. But what does his medication have to do with the murder?"

"Do you recall our conversation about GHB with Dr. Molinier? He mentioned that it was the

first pharmacological anti-depressant. Other med-
ications have replaced it, but it's finding favor
again in some psychiatric circles."

"And?"

"And I happened to get my hands on one of
Lee's capsules. I intend to find out if his 'new' anti-
depressant is GHB."

24

Benjamin brushed his teeth and smoothed his hair as he went over the multiple angles in Simone's drugging and death. He and Virgile had returned to their rooms after finishing their Cognacs. The winemaker had planned to check in with Jacqueline, his secretary in Bordeaux. He was too preoccupied, however, to tend to business. He finished freshening up and ordered tea. When his cell phone rang, he was tempted to let it go to voicemail. But then he saw who it was.

"Mr. Cooker, I had that capsule analyzed," Dr. Molinier said. "It's a selective serotonin reuptake inhibitor that the National Agency for the Safety of Medicines and Health Products approved last year."

"It's not GHB?"

"No, Mr. Cooker. I'm aware that some doctors are prescribing GHB again, but the SSRIs are much more common and, in my opinion, more effective. There's something else you may want to know."

"Tell me, please."

"As it turns out, they did perform an autopsy, and it was done right away, because the medical staff was suspicious. Heroin was found in Simone's bloodstream, Mr. Cooker. They think someone injected it directly into her IV line."

Benjamin gasped. "Heroin? It was heroin that finally did her in?"

"It appears to be the case. Simone was murdered at the hospital, just as she was recovering."

His hand shaking, Benjamin ended the call. Although he was relieved that Lee Friedman was no longer implicated, he was in shock. Benjamin sat down on his bed.

A moment later, Virgile knocked and came in. "Hungry, boss? I could use some lunch. My stomach's a bit unsettled after your news and the drink so early in the day. Maybe we could finally go to the Grand Vatel. I hear the Vatel salad with foie gras, gizzards, dried duck breast..." He stopped. "What's wrong, boss? Not more bad news, I hope."

Benjamin looked up at his assistant. "Virgile, I just spoke with Dr. Molinier. Someone injected Simone's IV line with heroin. That's why she went into respiratory arrest."

Virgile's chin dropped. Speechless, he plopped down on the bed next to Benjamin.

After a few minutes, the winemaker got up and walked toward the door. "I need to clear my head."

Virgile followed. "Where are we going?"

Without answering, Benjamin marched downstairs and outside. He got into the car and waited for his assistant to join him. As he drove out of the parking lot and onto the highway, he took deep breaths to calm himself. He began to relax as he accelerated.

Finally, he glanced at Virgile. "Have you seen Château du Clos Lucé, where Leonardo da Vinci spent the final three years of his life?"

"No, can't say that I have, although I've heard about it."

"Leonardo took up residence there at the invitation of King François I. To get to France, he crossed the Alps on a mule, carrying three of his masterpieces, *The Virgin and Child With Saint Anne*, *Saint John the Baptist*, and the *Mona Lisa*," which he was still perfecting. He wasn't a young man, Virgile. He was sixty-four."

"The king must have offered quite an incentive to make him do that," Virgile said.

"Leonardo was always in need of benefactors, and François promised a stipend and a home. While he lived at the Clos Lucé, Leonardo worked on several projects for the king, who was a great admirer. In fact, the king called Leonardo 'father.' He used a tunnel from his palace, the Château Royal d'Amboise, to visit the master. But our time is limited today, and it's the gardens that I want to see."

They made the short drive to Amboise, parked, and went straight to the grounds, which showcased life-sized inventions inspired by Leonardo's sketches. It was a balmy day, and the landscape was lush.

"This is called Leonardo's open-air museum, son. It's where you can envision the self-taught innovator, engineer, and architect, who observed nature and used it as his inspiration. Here, among the cypresses, pines, and blossoming plants, you can see the world through his eyes. Even the water comes to life. Look up, Virgile. Suspended in the trees above us are forty translucent canvasses. The models, meanwhile, are all hands-on and made with materials that would have been available during his life."

Three children scampered past the winemaker and his assistant. Giggling, they climbed aboard an assault chariot. They scrambled off and moved on to the multi-barreled gun, another invention they could work themselves. On the lake, teenagers propelled the Leonardo boat.

"Over there, Virgile, you can see the twenty-meter-high double-deck bridge. It was his way of improving urban traffic and hygiene. The lower level was for commercial traffic, while the top was for cleaner traffic."

"This place is almost magical, boss, like a fifteenth-century *Star Wars*."

Benjamin smiled. He was beginning to feel like his old self. "You're a fan, son?"

"Of course. A light saber was my all-time favorite Christmas present."

Benjamin stopped in his tracks. "Star Wars," he said.

"What about it, boss?"

"I just remembered an item I read in *Le Monde*. It seems Disney's set to collect fifty million dollars because Carrie Fisher died before *The Last Jedi* was completed. She'd signed a three-picture deal."

Virgile stepped aside for a couple approaching from behind. "I read about that too. But how's it connected to Leonardo da Vinci?"

"It has to do with the way we've been seeing things, son. Our vision has been off. We've assumed that the perpetrator in the Simone Margerolle case was acting out of revenge, anger, or a sense of powerlessness. But what if it was about something else?"

"I'm not following."

"What if the perpetrator had something to gain by getting rid of Simone? What if greed was the motive?"

25

Benjamin was impatient to get to their destination, as it was all coming together. But as soon as they hit the traffic on the beltway, he knew it wouldn't be quick or easy. The winemaker hated driving in this aggressive city.

"I have no idea why we're rushing to Paris, boss," Virgile said, opening the passenger-side door at one of the city's endless red lights. "But you might as well let me take the wheel. You're too worked up to drive."

Benjamin didn't protest and traded places. He sat back as Virgile skillfully threaded the Mercedes from one lane to the next and then back again to make time. An hour later they were at their destination, the Open Air Productions studio in the eleventh arrondissement.

Virgile found an unexpected parking space in Le Square Gardette. They got out and walked across the park, with its charming music kiosk, profusion of trees and flowers, and boules courts. Miraculously protected from the commotion of the boulevards, this enclosed neighborhood was a hidden treasure in the heart of the capital. Benjamin let out a sigh.

The company's office, rented space in a former haberdashery on the Rue Saint Ambroise, was far from luxurious. A slim woman in her twenties was sitting by herself at an austere eighties-style reception desk. Two photos and a potted plant on her desk were the only decorations.

She rose when they came in and walked over to shake their hands. Benjamin glanced at Virgile. His assistant had noted her short black curls and sparkling green eyes. Before he knew it, Virgile was flirting with her and had managed to get her name: Natalia. She was of Portuguese descent and had been working at Open Air for just a few months. Benjamin pulled him by the sleeve, reminding him why they were there.

Natalia directed them down a narrow spiral staircase to the editing room. Liza was waiting for them.

"Ah, here are our two film stars, now," she said fondly, turning to a fiftyish man with red mustache and sturdy frame. "This is Henri, the engineer who's collaborating with me on the editing."

Henri nodded and tipped his black felt cap.

"He's not quite set up yet. We weren't expecting you until the beginning of the week, but we're accommodating people, aren't we, Henri?"

Once again, Henri nodded.

"He'll just need a few minutes," Liza said. "Why don't we slip out so he can get ready for us. May I get you a cup of tea, Mr. Cooker? And coffee for you, Virgile?

"Yes, we'd appreciate that," Benjamin answered. "And please, call me Benjamin."

Liza asked Natalia to get the tea and coffee and ushered the men into her office. Although it was spartan, one of the walls was filled with framed awards and certificates of achievement. Benjamin walked over and studied them.

"I've been wondering, Liza," he said. "You're clearly a very talented director. Have you ever considered doing films?"

"As a matter of fact, that was my dream when I was studying at USC's School of Cinematic Arts. George Lucas of *Star Wars* fame went there, you know. But even though I was able to land jobs in television—on some major shows, in fact—I could never make it in films. In Hollywood, female directors are marginalized.

I've heard that some male actors refuse to take directions from a woman."

"Unbelievable," Virgile said.

"So I've made my career in documentaries. I'm not complaining, mind you. This line of work suits me. I can educate and inform our viewers, as I am with your project."

Henri opened the door and stuck his head in. "We're ready for you."

"Shall we?" Liza said, getting up. She led the men to the editing room, where she pulled up chairs for her visitors. Natalia arrived with their refreshments, and they took their places in front of the expansive desk and multiple flat screens, with Henri at the helm.

Before he could do anything, Benjamin turned to Liza. "I realize what an imposition this is, but could we postpone the viewing of all the rushes? There's one set in particular that I need to see right away."

Liza stiffened. "But we hurried to put everything together so you could view it at a time that was convenient for you."

"I understand, Liza. I promise we'll be back as quickly as possible."

Liza sighed. "All right, Benjamin. What is it that you need to see?"

"The clips from the party at David Navarre's château. What do you have?"

"We have him shaking your hand and saying a few words to you. We also filmed him drinking, but his face is as red as the Philippe Alliet Vieilles Vignes they were serving that night."

"What else?"

"Let's take a look."

Henri turned to the control panel and brought up the clips. Benjamin watched the servers, wearing the masks of perfectly trained minions as they made their way around sweaty dancers brought in from a modeling school, while hipsters mingled shamelessly with wheeler dealers who looked more like car salesmen than movie moguls. A few naïve-looking souls, meanwhile, wandered here and there. The ear-shattering tech music drowned out any dialogue.

Virgile came into view. He was dancing with Simone. As she laughed and chugged her Champagne, the camera panned the scene: the buffet table, the courtyard, a couple making out, and a singer about to vomit in a Medici vase. Back in the ballroom, several young actors were arguing.

Dr. Molinier and his wife, probably ready to call it a night, were looking bored. And David was drinking—staggering a few minutes later into the arms of a reality-show host. The camera swung to Simone again. Now she was playfully sticking out her tongue at a friend.

"Stop! You see that young man with gelled hair slinking between the dancers, his tray raised above their heads?" Benjamin said, pointing to the screen in earnest. "Go back, not too far. There! No, right there. Stop!"

"What about the guy?" Virgile asked, frowning. "What's so interesting?"

"That's not a guy, Virgile. That's a woman. And I know who she is."

"What are you talking about, boss?"

"I'll tell you shortly, son." He turned to Henri. "Could you zoom in and print out the image? I'd also like you to play with it a bit, if you could."

The engineer swiveled around in his chair. "Sure. Whatever you need."

Benjamin huddled with him briefly, standing over his shoulder and once again pointing to the large screen.

"Just give me a few minutes," Henri said after he knew exactly what Benjamin was asking for.

When he had finally worked his wizardry, Liza Stechelmann gasped. "That's Mathilde Desloges. What was she doing at David's party?"

"As you can see, she was passing herself off as someone else. But she made a fatal misstep. Can you tell me more about her?"

"As far as I know, she got her start in an appliance commercial. And then she landed a small role in a limited-run television series. After that, she attended the international drama school, Cours Florent, in Paris. She went on to stage productions but didn't manage to win any major roles in film or television. To tell the truth, I don't understand why such a good-looking and talented young actress never managed to land a star-making part."

"As it happens, her acting stint as a server didn't work out either."

26

"I'll be in Tours in two hours. I need to meet with you." Benjamin heard nothing at the other end of the call.

Finally, Inspector Blanchet spoke. "It's late, Mr. Cooker, and I'm tired. I was just putting on my coat to leave the office."

Benjamin could imagine the inspector's frustration and fatigue. The Simone Margerolle investigation had taken one bad turn after the other, and the papers and their websites were full of questions—questions for which the police had no answers. Had they assigned the right people to the case? Did they have the wherewithal to find the perpetrator? Most likely, Blanchet was resigning himself to working with the vice squad in Paris.

"We'll meet tomorrow," Blanchet said.

"No, Inspector, it has to be right away."

"I don't understand, boss," Virgile said, trailing the winemaker as he raced toward the car. "How did you figure out the Mathilde Desloges angle, and what does she have to do with Princess Leia?"

Benjamin slid into the driver's seat and waited for Virgile. "It's about greed, son, as I said. Who stood to gain from Simone's death? The young woman who'd replace her if she died. At David's party, I spilled wine on a male server. When I looked at the stain on his shirt, it occurred to me that there was something wrong. He was wearing a woman's shirt. But I was too embarrassed about my blunder to give it any thought."

"How did you know it was a women's shirt?"

"Men's dress shirts don't have darts at the bosom, Virgile. But more important, they button on the right side, not the left."

"I never realized that, boss. Why do men's and women's shirts button on different sides?"

"Historically, clothing for wealthy men included provisions for weaponry. Because most men held their swords in their right hands, it was more convenient to unbutton with their left. The image of the server in the women's dress shirt came back to me during our walk in the park."

"But Mathilde's masquerading as a man isn't enough to convict her for murder."

"You're right, son. There's more to it."

Benjamin and Virgile arrived at the police station and hurried to Blanchet's office on the first floor. The winemaker wasn't surprised to find the exhausted inspector slumped in his chair. He handed Blanchet the evidence that Henri had printed out.

"What's all that?" the inspector asked.

"What I've just given you will help you sleep peacefully," Benjamin answered.

"Well, shit! Let's take a look!"

Blanchet took the photos out of the manila envelope. Henri had skillfully erased the mustache, smoothed the cheekbones, outlined the lips, applied light makeup, and replaced the gelled men's wig with a long mane to reveal Mathilde, the gorgeous young woman with the enticing mole near her lip.

"Who is it?" Blanchet asked.

"I'll tell you very soon, but I have a request."

Blanchet frowned. "You may be used to getting your way in the circles you run in, Mr. Cooker, but they're not my circles."

"I understand, Inspector. But it's not a request that will put you out too much. I need to see the hospital's security tapes."

"I suppose you're not going to reveal why."

"That I'll also tell you—very soon."

The inspector sighed. "All right, Mr. Cooker. I know you have a reputation for solving crimes, and, to be frank, I could use a hand. Just don't tell the people in vice that you helped me."

"Deal," Benjamin said.

Blanchet made a phone call, and Benjamin and Virgile drove to the hospital. Two days were crucial: the day after Simone's arrival, and the day of her death. A hospital technician set everything up, and the winemaker and his assistant sat down.

"Boss, now that I'm thinking of it, there was a woman in Simone's room who looked like Mathilde. She had blond hair in a ponytail, and she was wearing scrubs. But her back was turned to me. She didn't say anything and left the room as soon as I came in."

"Most likely she was there to check on Simone's condition," Benjamin said.

Benjamin zeroed in on footage captured at the hospital entrance close to the time Virgile arrived. They saw Fabrice come in, and then an attractive blond woman wearing a hat, jeans, and sneakers.

"That's her!" Virgile said. "Mathilde!"

"Yep, that's our actress," Benjamin said. "She must have ducked into a locker room and slipped into scrubs."

A few minutes later, Virgile entered, and Fabrice left. Then Mathilde.

"All right," Benjamin said. "We've placed her at the hospital the day after Simone was admitted. Now let's go through the footage on the day Simone died."

Sure enough, they found her, this time wearing a floppy hat and sundress, entering the hospital close to the time of Simone's death. Not an hour later, she hurriedly left the facility through the same door.

"What was the time of Simone's death, boss?"

"Dr. Molinier said it was 6:53."

"Well, here she is, coming in at 6:16 and leaving at 7:05."

27

Virgile yawned as he leaned back in his seat. "Too much driving, boss. We didn't get back to Château de Pray till after eight last night. And now we have to hit the road again."

"I know, son. But we're almost there."

Benjamin had called Jean-Paul Gayraud that morning, asking for an appointment at his office in Paris on the pretext of doing the documentary they had discussed earlier, this one for a French audience.

"I'd love to meet with you, Benjamin," Gayraud had answered. "But I'll be tied up with Mathilde all day. We're going over the details of her role in Armond's movie. I'm heartsick about Simone, but I'm sure Mathilde will do a great job. I'm heading to her place right now. Can we make time to talk next week?"

"Certainly," Benjamin had responded, making an appointment he had no intention of keeping.

Now they were parked outside Mathilde's building on Avenue Henri-Martin, waiting for her to return from a jog. They watched as she rounded the corner and entered her first-floor apartment.

When she opened the door to them, Benjamin introduced himself as a friend of David Navarre's but added that he also knew Jean-Paul Gayraud.

At the mention of Gayraud, Mathilde raised an eyebrow. "So why are you here to see me?"

"It's a private matter," Benjamin said, slipping past her and stepping into her living room. He motioned to Virgile.

"You've got a lot of nerve," Mathilde said, an affronted look on her face as she watched Virgile join Benjamin. "What makes you think you can just waltz right in here?"

"'Waltz.' That's an intriguing word you just used, Miss Desloges. As a matter of fact, we have video footage of you waltzing into the hospital in Tours. First, the day after Simone Margerolle was admitted and again the day she was murdered."

"Murdered? Who said that?"

"According to the forensics examiners, Simone suffered respiratory arrest after she was administered heroin."

"That's horrible!" Mathilde said.

Benjamin had to hand it to her. With her talent, she should have made it further.

He heard a key turn in the door.

"*Ma chérie,* I tried to call you, but you weren't picking up." Gayraud came in and threw his keys on the bureau. Then he saw Benjamin and Virgile. "What a surprise, Benjamin. I thought we were meeting next week. And why are you here, at Mathilde's place?"

"You bring us here, Jean-Paul. That is, both you and Miss Desloges. We wanted you to know she won't be taking that part, after all."

"No?"

"No. She'll be in jail. For that matter, you'll be in jail too."

"What are you talking about?"

"I've put everything together. Actually, Virgile helped me, during a little stroll through the Leonardo da Vinci outdoor museum. Have you been there? It's really quite lovely. But I'm straying. It all started with the insurance policy you took out on Simone. It didn't take you long to realize there was much to gain if she didn't complete her film: not only the money you'd pocket, but also your girlfriend's undying affection. Was she growing unhappy with you, Jean-Paul? Were you unable to help her as much as you'd promised? With a reputation like yours, it's hard to make friends, isn't it. The offers weren't coming in. So you decided—and forgive me for putting it this way—to kill two birds with one stone. You'd collect on the insurance and please your girlfriend."

"That's a bit of a stretch, don't you think, Benjamin? Taking out insurance on a star—that's done every day. How does it prove anything?"

"By itself, it doesn't," Benjamin said. "When Inspector Blanchet arrives, and that should be any minute now, we'll sort everything out. He's already sent officers to your home. They'll search your place, confiscate your computer, trace your order for the GHB, and reconstruct your scheme. You and Mathilde plotted to slip the GHB into Simone's drink. You had Mathilde do it herself—and I must hand it to you, Jean-Paul, you left the party early to avoid incriminating yourself. Mathilde, in server's disguise, slipped the GHB into one of Simone's drinks. Then, with Simone lingering in the hospital, you showed up at David's place and set us up to select Mathilde as her replacement. But to your surprise, Simone didn't die. She actually started improving. So you moved on to Plan B. You added heroin to the mix, with Mathilde once again doing the dirty work.

Gayraud mopped his brow. "The heroin wasn't my idea. In fact, none of it was—not the disguise, not the binder, not the drugs, nothing. It was her, all her." He pointed to Mathilde.

Mathilde stared at her lover, disgust written all over her face. "I can't believe you. You'd actually pin the whole thing on me?" She turned to Benjamin and Virgile. "What a douchebag. What a stinking, worthless douchebag." She slumped against the bureau and sighed. "It was both of us. Now what?"

"Now we wait for the inspector," Benjamin said.

"I guess I should call my attorney," Jean-Paul said, pulling out his phone. He looked over at Mathilde. "Do you want me to give them your credit card information, sweetheart? I don't think my wife will let me pay for both of us."

$$\mathcal{S}\,\mathcal{S}\,\mathcal{S}$$

Seated on the terrace of Le Noailles on the Allées de Tourny, Benjamin Cooker and Virgile

Lanssien had just finished placing their lunch orders: veal liver for the winemaker and sole for his assistant.

"Boss, I don't think we've ever encountered a case as complicated as the last one. Simone Margerolle was betrayed by the producer of her movie, who connived with his girlfriend to murder her because he wanted the insurance money, and she wanted the part. But before that, Simone's insecure lover seduced another man's wife. And to get even, the husband tried to bed Simone. That didn't go so well. And then there was the skeleton, which once belonged to a man murdered by his very own cousin, who was scheming to get his hands on a piece of land that may or may not be jinxed."

Benjamin's smile turned to a frown when he felt his phone vibrate. Why was it that people always called when he was trying to do something else? He especially disliked taking calls when he was eating—on a warm and pleasant day, no less. But again, he answered.

The winemaker put the phone to his ear and listened as Inspector Blanchet thanked him. "It was no trouble at all, Inspector. And if you're ever in Bordeaux, please let me know."

Benjamin put the phone in his pocket and turned back to Virgile. Just then, it vibrated again.

He sighed, answered, spoke a few words, and said good-bye. "That was Elisabeth. She wants me to make a stop on my way home, which reminds me: I was just talking with Margaux. She's joined a cycling club, and she recently posted a picture on Instagram of herself with her girlfriend's fiancé. The three of them were cycling somewhere in upstate New York. She wound up deleting the photo because she thought a few people might have gotten the wrong idea. I'm a Facebook man myself, but you have an Instagram account, don't you, Virgile?"

"Yeah, I do." Virgile answered, moving a piece of sole around on his plate. Even though Virgile's head was bent over his fish, Benjamin couldn't miss the grin.

Benjamin cleared his throat. "I digress. Getting back to your thoughts on our exceptionally complicated case, I think Colette would sum it up much better than I."

"Is this Colette a friend of yours?"

"Don't be silly, Virgile. I'm talking about the writer Sidonie-Gabrielle Colette."

"I don't know what she would say, boss—or has said—but I have a feeling you're dying to tell me."

"'The lovesick, the betrayed, and the jealous all smell alike.'"

Epilogue

Simone Margerolle's memorial service took place a few weeks later, after her private burial in Paris. The arrest of Simone's replacement, along with her producer boyfriend, had put work on Max Armond's movie seriously behind schedule. Simone's few family members, who lived in Ireland, had agreed to delay the service to accommodate the director.

The church was crowded with somberly dressed celebrities. In turn, they stepped up to give their remembrances, while also promoting their most recent projects: a play, a film, a television appearance... Benjamin couldn't help feeling sad for the young woman who, despite the orchestrated and choreographed memorial production, was already forgotten. Only David Navarre seemed sincere. With dignity, he talked about her talent and her love of life.

"I have so many regrets, Benjamin," he said after everyone had poured from the church and gotten into their limos. "I loved Simone and didn't show her the way I should have. I should have taken on Armond and given her more attention. If I had, she wouldn't have looked for it elsewhere. And if I hadn't been so drunk that night…"

"You mustn't do that to yourself," Benjamin said. "If they hadn't drugged her, they would have found another opportunity. You had no way of knowing." Benjamin changed the subject in an attempt to cheer him up. "I'm looking forward to working with you on your vineyard. I'll be there soon, along with Virgile. And I'm pleased you didn't allow yourself to buy into the notion that the parcel's jinxed."

For the first time that day, the actor smiled. "Have I ever looked like a superstitious man, Benjamin? And I already have a name for the cuvée. 'Invincible.' If all goes well, we'll have the jewel of Château de Tremblay."

"We'll do our best, David. Thank goodness this is one production that won't be filmed."

"Right," David said. "No cameras allowed." He fell silent for a moment. "Benjamin, I can't get over Lee Friedman's death, and so soon after Simone. Did you go to the funeral?"

"Yes. His family wanted to keep it private, but they made an exception for me. I don't know why."

Lee Friedman had committed suicide, swallowing a host of meds in one go. His cleaning woman had found him the morning after, his face resting on the keyboard of his computer. A Mavis Staples recording, "I'll Take You There," was playing in a loop.

"It's hard to understand," David said. "He'd just signed a contract for another screenplay. The producers wanted me to star in it, but unfortunately, I had to decline. I'd heard, though, that several other big names were interested."

"Why didn't you want the part?" Benjamin asked.

"I'm retiring."

Benjamin was taken aback. "But you still have so many major roles ahead of you. Surely you'll miss acting."

"No, I won't. I'm done with it. I plan to give all my attention to my vineyards and enjoy a nice quiet life out of the spotlight."

Benjamin spotted Virgile walking over to join them.

"Well, kid, I understand I'll be seeing a lot of you in the next few months," David said.

Benjamin couldn't help noticing that his assistant's smile looked forced. He sensed that Virgile was relieved that Margaux hadn't given her heart to someone else. She was and would be his true love. Still, the boy had been affected by Simone Margerolle, the beautiful actress who had appeared—almost like an illusion—and lingered for no more than a few minutes before vanishing.

"Yes, I'll be there," Virgile answered.

Benjamin could see Virgile wasn't in the mood to chat. He turned to David. "I hear you'll soon be done with your movie. Will you be at the premiere?"

"No, Benjamin. As I said, I'm retiring. No more premieres for me. By the way, I've given up the whiskey, too. I was drinking way too much. I'm sorry I didn't do it earlier."

Benjamin and Virgile said their good-byes and headed toward the winemaker's convertible. Benjamin glanced at his assistant, who still seemed pensive.

"You all right, son?"

"Yeah, boss, I'm okay. But I have a request. I know we have work to do in the lab, but if you don't mind, I'd like to get back to the vineyards right away."

"I suppose we could do that. We need to make appointments with several estate owners. We could put the lab work off. May I ask why?"

"Well, to tell the truth, I've been feeling a little strange lately, like nothing's what it seems. Maybe it's because of all the time we've spent with movie types, whose aim is creating what's essentially a fabrication. Not that I have anything against a good film. It's just that only the grapes and vines seem real to me right now. They're calling me, boss. I need some dirt under my nails to feel grounded."

Thank you for reading

Foul play in Vouvray

Please share your thoughts and reactions on your favorite social media and retail platforms.

DON'T MISS THE OTHER TITLES IN THE

WINEMAKER DETECTIVE SERIES

Treachery in Bordeaux
Grand Cru Heist
Nightmare in Burgundy
Deadly Tasting
Cognac Conspiracies
Mayhem in Margaux
Flambé in Armagnac
Montmartre Mysteries
Backstabbing in Beaujolais
Late Harvest Havoc
Tainted Tokay
Red-Handed in Romanée-Conti
Requiem in Yquem

Want to read more for free?
Read your way to France
Get your discovery pack:
www.lefrenchbook.com/read-your-way-to-france

Printed in Great Britain
by Amazon